The Silver Tree

The Silver Tree

by Ruth L. Williams

A Charlotte Zolotow Book

An Imprint of HarperCollins*Publishers*

For information address HarperCollins Children's Books, a division of HarperCollins Publishers, 10 East 53rd Street, New York, NY 10022.
Typography by Joyce Hopkins
1 2 3 4 5 6 7 8 9 10
First Edition

Library of Congress Cataloging-in-Publication Data
Williams, Ruth L.
    The silver tree / by Ruth L. Williams.
        p.   cm.
    "A Charlotte Zolotow book."
    Summary: Micki Silver must go back in time to stop a wish she has made from coming true—one that could destroy her family.
    ISBN 0-06-020296-3. — ISBN 0-06-020297-1 (lib. bdg.)
    [1.   Space and time—Fiction.]   I.   Title.
PZ7.W66817Si 1992   91-16399
[Fic]—dc20   CIP
                                                                                         AC

For Murray, the
greatest Great-uncle

Contents

The Silver Tree

1

The Toy Museum

When Micki awoke on the first Saturday of her two-week spring vacation and looked out the window, her heart fell. The April rain was beating down in fast little pellets against the glass pane, and the gray clouds that hovered low above the dripping trees looked as if they meant business.

"Oh no!" she groaned. "What about the picnic?"

"It doesn't look like there's going to be any picnic." It was Mrs. Silver, Micki's mother, who was standing in the bedroom doorway. "We'll just have

to have it another time," she added sympathetically.

"But Mother, you and Daddy *promised*! You said
we'd go *today*!"

"Now honey, I can't very well help the weather,
can I? Come on, cheer up, there's lots of things we
can do on a rainy day. We'll think of something."

But the rain had put Micki in a sour mood. Even
though she knew better, she couldn't help thinking that if her mother had really put her mind to it,
she could have done something about the gloomy
weather. Grownups were like that sometimes.
They pleaded innocence and refused to admit
they had certain powers. She wrenched the bedclothes right up to her face so that only her nose
and eyes peeked out.

"But I don't want to do something else; I want
to go on a picnic," grumbled Micki. Her mother
said nothing, but she gave her daughter one of
those powerful disapproving looks which made
Micki feel even madder.

Micki dressed as slowly as she could. She put on
her red-and-white-striped T-shirt and a pair of
paisley pants because they were the worst combination she could find. She looked in the mirror and
scowled. Her long brown hair was stringy and
knotted, as it always was in the morning. But today
she didn't brush it because she knew it would

annoy her mother.

After her father had called her twice to the breakfast table, she decided to go downstairs. She dragged her feet lazily along the steps, kicking the banister as she went and making such great thumping noises that her father came to the bottom landing and stared up at her severely.

"Young lady, if you don't come down here at once and take that sullen look off your face, there won't be any pancakes for you this morning," he said, shaking his spatula up at her. He appeared very formidable in his white apron all splattered with grease and batter.

Micki did not glance up when she entered the kitchen. She just sat down at the table and stared glumly at the two perfect golden-brown pancakes on her plate. They looked delicious all covered with melted butter and warm maple syrup. But Micki pretended to have no interest in her favorite breakfast. She was mad, mad, mad. When her six-year-old little sister, Jenny, tugged at her arm in joyous excitement, she just shrugged her off roughly.

"Micki, Micki, Mommy and Daddy are taking us to the *toy* museum today!" Jenny burst out. Her face was flushed with anticipation, and she bounced up and down in her chair gaily. "Toys, toys, toys!" she chanted, glowing with happiness and oblivious to everyone else at the breakfast table.

"I don't *want* to go to some old toy museum," Micki replied loudly. And then, because she thought Jenny had no right to be happy when she was feeling so irritable and rotten, she said viciously, "I thought you wanted to go on a picnic, Jenny, and now you want to go see a bunch of stupid toys. Why can't you make up your mind?"

Jenny looked at her sister guiltily, as if she had betrayed her without knowing how.

"But Micki," she said in a timid little voice, "it's raining, and besides, Mommy says . . ."

"Mommy says, Mommy says," Micki mimicked cruelly, dashing out of the kitchen before her father had a chance to tell her to march straight up to her room and that there would be no pancakes for a certain young lady this morning because of the totally uncalled-for behavior with which she had graced the breakfast table.

Micki's father gave her the choice of saying she was sorry and coming along or staying at home with a baby-sitter. There was little that Micki loathed quite so much as being left at the mercy of a baby-sitter. The last one they'd had made her and Jenny stay downstairs in the living room and watch television game shows so that she could "keep an eye on them." Besides, Micki thought, eleven was far too old for baby-sitters. So she mumbled a half-hearted apology to Jenny and her parents, climbed sullenly into the backseat of the car, and proceeded to stare out the window, her arms folded defensively in front of her.

Micki certainly didn't feel apologetic. If anything, she was madder than before. She wouldn't even look at her sister, who for some reason made her angrier than anyone else. Jenny's curious, slightly fearful, sidelong glances were almost more than she could bear.

"If only I were an orphan," she thought spitefully, "and an only child—then no one could bother me or tell me what to do."

The windshield wipers slapped rhythmically back and forth above the dashboard, sweeping aside the rain that spattered onto the glass. Everything looked gray and dirty as the car sped past the somber houses with their unfriendly shuttered windows. Huge puddles had collected alongside the road, and some of the sewers were so clogged with mud and leaves that the streets had almost become rivers.

Micki watched the pedestrians plunging their umbrellas against the wind. The car hurtled past an old lady struggling with a shopping cart and a hopelessly inside-out umbrella, drenching her with filthy water. Micki found the sight unusually funny, and for the first time that day she broke into a smile, and then into a laugh. It was not a nice laugh. In fact, it sounded so strange that at first Micki did not realize that it was she who was laughing.

The toy museum was a place that Mr. Silver had discovered one Sunday morning when he was wandering about the back alleyways of the old section of the city, peering into crowded antique shop windows, looking for one of his famous "bargains." He was walking about aimlessly, when suddenly he came across a small street he had never seen before. He followed it nearly to the end when he glanced up and saw a warped wooden sign scrawled with faded, hand-painted lettering that read "Madame F's Toy Museum."

Mr. Silver loved making discoveries. It was a quality that endeared him to his two daughters and caused his wife a certain degree of frustration. Without thinking twice, he yanked open the heavy oak door and began bounding up the stairs of the decrepit old house. Up and up he ran, until he was quite short-winded.

Strange, he thought, surely the building was only three stories high. But still more flights rose above him. He ascended more slowly, stopping every once in a while to catch his breath. Finally he reached the top landing, which was dimly lit by a grimy skylight. He then came face to face with a huge doorway upon which another hand-painted sign was posted, identical to the one outside the building.

He knocked, gently at first, and then, when there was no answer, more loudly. After what seemed like an unusually long time—in fact Mr. Silver had turned to go—there was a heavy creaking noise, and the door opened just enough to reveal two large brown eyes peering out of an incredibly wrinkled face. Beyond the face, Mr. Silver could dimly make out in the shadowy light row upon row of objects reaching way up to the ceiling. Toys! Never had he seen so many toys, and they were probably only the beginning.

"Yes?" a voice inquired sharply. Mr. Silver realized that the old woman (for the face was, indeed, a woman's, although so ancient that it was difficult to tell) was having to repeat herself.

"I would like to see the museum," he said, somewhat surprised. It seemed obvious why he had come.

"Where are the children?" the voice demanded, and the crack in the doorway narrowed slightly, so that everything inside was obscured.

"Excuse me?" asked Mr. Silver, not comprehending.

"The children," repeated the voice. "Please read the sign." Mr. Silver scrutinized the notice on the door more closely. "Madame F's Toy Museum," it read, and then, below it, in tiny letters that he had failed to observe before: "No Adults Admitted Without Children."

The woman stared at him with grave disapproval, and he felt like a schoolboy who had done poorly on a very easy test. He gazed back into the huge, dark, unblinking eyes, and just for a brief moment he had the strange sensation that he had seen them somewhere before. Then the door snapped shut in his face, and he was left staring at the hand-painted sign. "Madame F's Toy Museum," it read. Nothing more.

Mr. Silver's curiosity did not let him forget the toy museum, but he kept it to himself. For weeks the memory nestled in the back of his mind, and it was not until this rainy Saturday morning that it emerged again—what a wonderful place to take Micki and Jenny to make up for the promised, but doomed, picnic! He was almost as excited by the prospect as Jenny. He was hurt by Micki's stubborn and thoughtless opposition.

"I'll bet when she gets there she'll change her tune, though," he said to himself, remembering the huge array of toys stretching back into the depths of the darkened museum.

Mr. Silver had a good deal of trouble finding the museum again. For some reason its exact location eluded him, but he knew it was somewhere hidden amid the complex web of alleyways. When they finally arrived, the building seemed even more gray and forlorn than he remembered it. Micki's mother looked up at the sign and glanced skeptically at her husband, but he pretended not to notice.

"Are you sure this is wise, Robert?" she asked as they began the long climb to the top. Mrs. Silver's common sense—which her children, and occasionally their father, were inclined to view as lack of sportsmanship—made her question this latest whim of her husband's. After all, was this really a good idea, dragging the family up to the attic of a slummy-looking building that was no doubt, among other things, an incredible fire hazard?

"I told you, Louise, I've been here before. It's perfectly all right." Already a flight ahead, he shouted this half-truth down to his wife and continued his rapid ascent. He was waiting for them when they arrived at the top, panting and out of breath, Micki bringing up the reluctant rear. Her mood had not changed, and her face remained a mask of sullenness. Her father glanced at her with a hurt expression, his excitement checked by his

11

daughter's lack of enthusiasm. But Micki pointedly ignored him and stared blankly at the heavy wooden door in front of them.

Micki's father knocked loudly, and after a wait of some minutes the door was opened by the tiniest and most wizened old woman Micki had ever seen. She had huge brown eyes that seemed to jump out from her face. The woman's gaze took in the Silver family huddled close together on the landing, and Micki felt the eyes (or was it simply her imagination?) flicker dimly with disapproval as they passed over her.

"Come in," said the woman in a voice that was unexpectedly deep and strong for someone so small. When the door swung open to admit them, Micki forgot her resolution to remain unimpressed and gasped in wonder. Never in her life had she seen so many toys! There were wooden dolls with painted faces, whole armies of tin soldiers, an entire menagerie of stuffed animals—dogs, cats, elephants, giraffes, exotic birds, foxes, bears, and some that Micki could not even identify—china tea sets, colored balls, spinning tops, piggy banks, paint sets with cracked lids, giant wooden building blocks, funny-looking bats and paddles, miniature cars and trucks, and way above, hanging from the old oak-beamed rafters, were three beautiful, brightly painted hobbyhorses.

Micki caught herself just in time. The black mood she was in could not be so easily shrugged off, she thought with a kind of ugly pride. She almost wished she could enjoy herself, but that would be like admitting she was wrong. And Micki hated being wrong. So she dragged her feet and entered the room behind the rest of the family.

Her parents were paying the admission fee.

"That's fifty times three and the little one for free. One fifty," said the old woman.

"Both girls are underage," corrected Micki's father politely.

"Age has nothing to do with it," the woman snapped. "Each according to his or *her* deserts." She threw such a look of disdain in Micki's direction that he paid the money at once.

The family shuffled uncomfortably into the enormous room—all except for Jenny, who was hugging herself and crooning gently.

Jenny's gaiety did little to improve Micki's dour spirits. Her face screwed up into an unattractive frown, and she was about to utter a scathing remark to her sister when she suddenly spied two huge disapproving eyes boring straight into her own. Micki lowered her head with a slight twinge of real shame. When she looked up again, the eyes had disappeared.

Micki glanced around the room at the rows of

beautiful playthings. They shone down on her with a pale incandescence, reaching out to her, almost whispering. But when she saw her parents watching her slyly, smiling at each other with knowing looks and pretending all the while not to notice her, Micki lapsed again into sulkiness.

"If only I could be alone," she thought, "I could *really* have a good time!" And then the idea occurred to her that perhaps when no one was looking, she could simply run off into one of the other rooms and have the place to herself. So when all heads were turned—her parents examining the rafters ("Funny, you'd never expect to see such a sturdy attic at the top of such a rundown-looking tenement," her mother was saying), her sister floating dreamily about the room—Micki slipped quietly through a side door.

She passed through several rooms without even looking. She wanted to get far, far away. But when she came to a room filled with automated toys, she stopped. Every corner of this small, low-ceilinged chamber was teeming with motion: miniature trains running through tunnels and up and around a tiny alpine mountain; fire engines that flashed red and raised little wooden ladders; a monkey scurrying up and down a painted palm tree eagerly collecting coconuts; a small dog that hurried back and forth barking silently and wagging its short stub of a tail; a red-coated soldier with a fur-trimmed cap strutting about and performing acts of military showmanship with a tiny polished rifle.

Micki stared and stared, trying to take it all in at once. She ran around the room lost in wonder, her anger swallowed up by an overpowering sense of awe. She felt as if she could stay here for hours and still not have enough. But it seemed only a matter of minutes before she heard voices.

"Micki, where are you?" called her mother.

Suddenly Micki was seized by a desperate desire to run. She cast about her, searching for a means of escape, and spying a small open doorway, she shot through it just as her parents entered the room from the other side.

Then she began to run. She ran through more rooms than she could ever have imagined such a narrow building could hold—and not once did she look behind her. At last, after she had been going on blindly for some time, Micki came to what seemed to be a dead end. She glanced around breathlessly and saw a small side door with a sign that read "PRIVATE" nailed to the inner paneling.

Without thinking twice, Micki wrenched the door open and burst headlong into an empty room.

2

The Dollhouse

The room was quite long but appeared to be nestled under the corner of an attic eave. At the far end the roof slanted down so low that even Jenny could not have stood her full height beneath it. The room was unlit except for one small oval window that admitted a bright shaft of sunlight. Tiny particles of dust floated lazily about, glinting like gold inside the warmth of the sunbeam.

"That's odd," Micki thought. "It was raining like crazy just a few minutes ago."

A jumble of empty cardboard boxes piled up alongside both walls suggested that the room had little practical use other than as a place to throw rubbish.

"What's so private about a bunch of dirty old boxes?" Micki muttered disappointedly. There was nothing here to see. But if she turned and went back the way she had come, she would be sure to run into her parents and Jenny, and they were the last people she wanted to see now. All any of them ever seemed to do was pick on her.

"I *wish* I'd never been born!" she shouted angrily, picking up a small stick that lay at her feet and snapping it in two. She kicked the pieces roughly across the room and watched as the broken branch skittered across the floor and bounced off a dark shape in the corner.

Micki squinted, shading her eyes against the sunlight that obscured her vision. What was that in the corner over there? She could make out only the vague rectangular lines of a strangely shaped box. She crossed the room slowly.

"Why, it's a house!" she exclaimed. It was a dollhouse. She ran toward it excitedly. From the outside the house was like no other dollhouse Micki had ever seen. First of all, it was very large for a dollhouse, the top window reaching nearly to her shoulders. And unlike the dollhouses that she and her friends were used to playing with, this one was not made of wood or metal or cardboard. It was made of real stone. Micki ran her fingers along the rough gray pebbles and across the perfectly crafted window ledges. She touched the tiny flowerpots ensconced in the windowbox on the second floor. Why, even the little red geraniums looked real!

But there was something else about this doll-house that was different. Something was missing.

"What's wrong?" Micki asked herself, stepping back to get a better view of the whole house. Then she snapped her fingers. Of course! The front of the house was completely enclosed! There was no way to *play* with this dollhouse.

"How weird," Micki murmured. "Now what's the point of a dollhouse that no one can get their hands into? Unless the front of the house has some kind of hinge so that you can take off the front when you want to play." She drew closer to the house, feeling along the edge for a hidden spring. Then she peered down into the uppermost oval window and caught her breath.

Inside was the most perfect miniature room she had ever seen. It was a tiny attic. It looked as if it might be some kind of combination bedroom-playroom. There were two single beds at one end of the room draped with white lacey-looking covers. Two dark-colored bureaus stood alongside another wall, each with an oval mirror attached by wooden struts that curved out from the back. The middle of the room was strewn with all sorts of toys, from stiff little china-faced dolls to brightly painted spinning tops. In one corner of the room stood a smiling hobbyhorse, in the other a tiny dollhouse.

"A dollhouse inside a dollhouse," she whispered. Suddenly the door burst open.

But it wasn't the door behind her. It was the one inside the dollhouse. And into the attic room galloped a little boy dressed in a dark-blue sailor suit with gold buttons, followed by a girl who appeared to be about Micki's age. Then all at once—though it seemed quite natural at the time—the dollhouse didn't look like a dollhouse anymore. It looked like a regular-sized room, and the children looked like regular-sized children. Micki felt just as though she were peering through the window of a house on her block.

The boy made straight for the hobbyhorse, climbed astride it, and began to rock furiously back and forth. The girl ran across the room, gathering up her long blue skirts so as not to trip over them. She flounced onto one of the beds and turned so that Micki could see the expression on her face. It was distinctly annoyed.

"Why, Matthew? Why do I have to share *my*

room with her? It's bad enough that I have to let you children use it as a playroom. Look at this mess you've made!"

The boy slowed down his rocking and looked disdainfully at the girl.

"It's not all *my* mess, Sarah. Those are Lizzie's dolls. And Mama says you have to share your room with Cousin Michelle because you're the same age. So *there!*" And he began rocking again violently.

Sarah raised her chin angrily, flipping back one of the tight blond braids that hung nearly to her waist.

"It's just not *fair*! No one asked her to come and stay with us. Gregory overheard Mama saying she'd been told Michelle was a simply horrid girl. I shan't have it! I shan't!"

"Sarah! That's dreadfully unkind of you." A girl of about thirteen had entered the room. She walked over to the other bed and sat demurely at the edge.

"Cousin Michelle lost both of her parents a year ago, and she has no brothers or sisters. She's a poor orphan and must feel terribly alone. Mother says we must be kind to her."

"Mother says, Mother says!" Sarah mimicked. "Mary, why do you always have to be such a little saint?"

"Where is Gregory?" asked Mary, ignoring her sister's remark. "He said he'd be here for our meeting. It's past two o'clock."

"Well, we can't very well start without him, since he called it," replied Sarah. "Does anyone know if he found out anything?"

Mary shook her head and Matthew stopped rocking. He glanced from Sarah to Mary with a look of importance.

"Yes," he said.

"Matthew! What did he say? Quick, tell us!" demanded Sarah. Both girls eyed their brother with obvious excitement. Matthew grinned at them impishly, enjoying the attention he was receiving.

"He didn't say. But I think," he said, lowering his voice to a dramatic whisper, "I think he saw *her* again."

Mary drew in her breath sharply and Sarah stared at her sister, wide-eyed.

"My goodness, that *is* news!" she exclaimed. "Oh I *do* wish he would hurry up. I can't wait to hear what he has to tell us!" She sprang up from the bed and ran to the window, impatiently pulling back the lace curtains.

"I wonder what those men are doing down there?" she mused aloud after a moment of silent gazing. "Mary, Matthew, come and see—it looks as if they're carrying something heavy."

But before the other children could reach the window, a small figure came bounding breathlessly into the room. It was a little girl, no more than four or five. Her eyes were round with fear, and she was on the verge of tears.

"Lizzie, what is it!" exclaimed Mary.

"Oh Sarah, Mary, come quick!" Lizzie pleaded. "It's Gregory—he's been hurt awful bad. He looks dead!"

The others stared at their sister in disbelief. Matthew was the first out the door. He leaped off the hobbyhorse so suddenly that it went careening into the wall, where it shuddered to a halt. The three girls stood for a moment, pale and trembling. Then, as if they were a single being, they turned and rushed from the room.

"Micki!" screamed a tiny voice. "Where are you?"

"I'm coming, Lizzie!" Micki called before she realized that the voice was Jenny's. She straightened up and glanced about her. The musty attic had not changed, except that the beam of sunlight was broader now and had begun to climb partway up the wall.

"Could I have been dreaming?" she muttered, shaking her head sharply back and forth. Micki

moved slightly, in silent conversation.

"Robert, what is it? Are you all right?" asked Micki's mother, peering anxiously at her husband.

Mr. Silver shrugged suddenly, and he seemed to be thrusting away some uncomfortable thought.

"What? Oh, did I miss something?" he said rather vaguely. "Isn't it about time we were going? Say, it looks as though the weather might have cleared up a bit," he added cheerfully, glancing at the sunlight streaming through the attic window.

The Silver family made their way slowly and quietly through the tangle of rooms until they again found themselves in the large entrance chamber of the museum. There was no one in sight. Micki's father reached for the heavy metal doorknob to usher out the family, and then jumped back in surprise when a deep voice sounded from behind them.

"Did you find what you were looking for?" the voice asked smoothly. It was the old woman. She had evidently been hidden somewhere in the shadowy recesses of the front room.

"We enjoyed ourselves very much," replied Mrs. Silver politely. "We wish we could stay longer," she added nervously.

"We can't always have what we wish for," said the old woman. "But then again, sometimes we can." She was staring pointedly at Micki as she made this cryptic remark. Micki squirmed uncomfortably under the harsh gaze of the woman's deep, brown eyes.

"Well, we'd best be going," said Micki's mother, attempting a bright conversational tone. "Thank you so much."

When the family had reached the ground floor of the old building and emerged into the open air, the rain was driving hard as ever against the gray pavement.

As Micki lay awake that night, the day's events seemed to swirl around confusedly in her brain.

She had been sent to bed early, since her mood had not improved. Her parents, too, seemed irritable, and she thought it best not to argue when her father beat her to it and told her to march straight up to her room.

Jenny made one last halfhearted attempt to make friends with Micki after she flounced angrily upstairs. But she fled in tears when Micki turned and snapped at her.

Right now Micki didn't want to think about herself. So instead she thought about the dollhouse and Sarah, Mary, Matthew, and Lizzie. And what about their brother Gregory? What had happened to him? She remembered Sarah looking out the window and seeing some men carrying something heavy. Micki felt a cold chill run down her spine and began biting her fingernails uneasily. They tasted unpleasantly gritty.

"Everything is so mixed up," she mumbled to herself as she began to drift into sleep.

When she had nearly dozed off, Micki thought she heard someone in her room. It sounded as if the person was rummaging through her bureau drawers. She imagined it must be her mother, but when she tried to call out to her, she found she couldn't speak or even move.

"I must already be asleep," she thought. "I'm dreaming." But she was sure her eyes were open. At first she could see no one. Then suddenly, on the wall across from her bed, she made out a vague shadow that became gradually clearer. It was a face hovering inside a kind of oval cloud above the bureau. The face was an old woman's, and Micki realized with a clutching terror that it was the old woman from the museum.

The woman's lips didn't move, but Micki could hear her words fill the room.

"Some of us do indeed get what we wish for," they sounded, and the huge, brown eyes seemed to be searching for Micki in the darkness. Micki still could not move. She could only stare help-lessly at the face until it slowly began to fade and shrink like a scene in an old movie.

The old woman's words seemed to reverberate as her face grew smaller and fainter.

"Wish for . . . wish for . . . wish for," they echoed.

Micki could feel her heart pounding hard against her chest. Then her eyes grew suddenly heavier, and try as she might to fight it, sleep descended like a black curtain.

3

A Rude Awakening

Sun was streaming through the window when Micki awoke the next morning. She could feel its warmth even before she opened her eyes, and she knew today she would be in a much better mood. She would even be nice to Jenny, she thought, brushing the bedclothes from her face. They felt strangely lacey.

Then she sat up in astonishment.

She wasn't in her own bed at all. Or in her own room.

She was in a large bedroom with a sloping roof. Next to her was an empty bed with covers that had obviously been tousled by much tossing and turning. Across the room was a wooden hobbyhorse that had been overturned against the far wall.

And then Micki knew, unmistakably, where she was. She was inside the dollhouse.

She swallowed nervously and felt something tight around her neck. She looked down and saw she was no longer wearing her comfortable cotton nightgown. Instead she had on a voluminous outfit with a high, starchy collar that was buttoned almost to her chin.

Before she could think about what to do next, the bedroom door opened, and in walked a girl about her own age wearing a dark blue pinafore over a frilly white dress that reached to just above her ankles. Her face was very pale.

"Good morning, Michelle," she said politely. "I'm Sarah. I hope I didn't wake you this morning, but you were still asleep, and I couldn't stay in bed any longer."

Michelle. Sarah thought she was her cousin Michelle. Until that moment, Micki had not made the connection between the name of the children's hateful cousin and her own real name.

"Where am I?" asked Micki cautiously.

Sarah looked at her with a quizzical expression.

"Don't you know? You're at our house in the country. You must have been fast asleep when they brought you here last night. I know I was. I didn't even hear them bring you in. I expect I was dreadfully tired staying up so late."

There was a pause. "My brother Gregory was in a terrible accident yesterday," Sarah said with a slight tremor in her voice.

Micki felt her heart skip a beat.

"What happened to him?" she asked.

"He fell from the maple tree outside our house. The branch he was sitting on just snapped underneath him. We still don't know how it happened. We've every one of us climbed that tree I don't know how many times, and the limbs have always been able to hold three of us at once. One of the workmen who saw him just before he fell said he wasn't even that high up."

Micki wanted to ask how Gregory was, but she was afraid of what the answer might be.

"He's very bad," said Sarah, as if reading her thoughts. "He's unconscious. They let me see him for a minute, and he was so white, I hardly knew him."

Micki was silent, so Sarah continued. She was trying unsuccessfully to hold back the tears.

"My parents won't tell us anything, except that everything is going to be all right. But I snuck up to the door when they were in there with the doctor, and I overheard him telling them that Gregory might not pull through. My mother hasn't left his side since."

Micki didn't know what to say. She thought she must be dreaming. But if she was, it was the most real dream she'd ever had, and there seemed to be no way of waking up.

In the meantime, here she was in a strange house, with a family that thought she was one of their relatives. There were other things that made Micki uncomfortable as well. For instance, why was Sarah wearing clothes that looked like something she'd seen in the illustrations of *Little Women*? And why was Micki wearing this strange, uncomfortable nightgown? The room, too, seemed as if it were from another era.

Even more worrisome to Micki was the thought of what would happen to her when the real cousin Michelle arrived, and the family found out they had been harboring a stranger. How would she be able to get back home then? For that matter, how could she get back home right now? Micki felt a sudden longing for her own room, and the comfort of her own family. And she thought guiltily of how yesterday had ended.

Then something inside her hardened. She had wanted to get away from her parents and her sister, and now here she was. She was determined to make the best of the situation, and even enjoy it if she could.

Sarah was brushing away her tears with the apron of her pinafore.

"I'm sorry," she said somewhat brusquely. "It's just that I'm so frightened for Gregory."

"Maybe he'll be all right," said Micki sympathetically.

"I don't know," said Sarah doubtfully. "But I'm sorry you had to come at a time like this. I hope you'll forgive everyone if they're not the best hosts. But that doesn't mean you can't have a nice breakfast," she added, brightening. "Cook has made something special in honor of your arrival."

For the first time Micki realized how hungry she was. She'd had no breakfast the day before, just a toasted cheese sandwich for lunch, and then she'd only picked at her dinner before being dismissed from the table.

"Why don't you start getting dressed, and I'll go and fetch you a washbasin. You'll find your clothes over there. They have already been put away." Sarah motioned to the bureau and the large wardrobe on Micki's side of the room. Then she turned and left the room.

Micki tossed aside the bedclothes and began undoing the endless buttons of her nightdress. She was eager to change into her comfortable jeans and a T-shirt. But when she opened her bureau drawer, her heart sank. There, stacked in neat little piles, were all manner of frilly blouses and woolen stockings. Micki ran to the closet and flung open the double doors. Five or six long flouncy dresses with oversmocks hung in a row on heavy wooden hangers. At the bottom of the closet were two pairs of the ugliest black lace-up boots she had ever seen.

Micki did her best to struggle into some semblance of an outfit. But she was at a loss to discover which piece of unfamiliar clothing to put on first. When Sarah returned to the room carrying a large pitcher and basin, she set them down on a small side table and stared at Micki with a look of puzzled amazement.

"Why, you've got the whole thing on backward!" she exclaimed. "Besides, wouldn't you like to wash first? Here, let me do it." She helped Micki step out of the oversmock, which she had put on before her dress. Then she took the heavy pitcher, poured its contents into the basin, and handed Micki a piece of toweling.

The water was freezing cold. It was as much as Micki could do to splash it on her face as Sarah looked on. She glanced about her for some soap, but seeing none, thought it best not to comment. The towel felt abrasive on her skin, and Micki finished washing as quickly as possible.

Before she knew what was happening, Sarah had popped a pale pink dress over her head and was lacing it up tightly from the back.

"Ow, I can't breathe!" Micki winced.

"Come now, Michelle," said Sarah somewhat impatiently. "Anyone would think you'd never worn a frock before! Here, put on your pinafore and your shoes, and let's go downstairs. I'm sure you must be starving!"

The house was so large and spacious that Micki found herself musing about why Sarah had been forced to share a room with her, and why their bedroom had to double as a playroom for the younger children. But she didn't have much time to spend wondering, because she knew she had to keep her wits about her. Wisely, she thought it best to say as little as possible until she knew more about her newfound cousin and her family.

Breakfast was delicious. The rest of the family had apparently already eaten, for they were nowhere in sight. A woman in a black dress and starched white apron brought in a tray and set out a plate of shirred eggs and thick round slabs of bacon for each of the two girls. There were freshly baked black currant muffins with melted butter and cups of steaming, frothy hot chocolate. Micki thought the muffins were perfect—even better than her father's pancakes.

Sarah was quiet all through breakfast. Her face wore an expression of discontentment, and she barely touched her food. There was no evidence of the friendliness she had shown earlier. It was as if she had exhausted her hostess repertoire and had lapsed into the rather petulant girl whom Micki had seen the day before. Micki felt distinctly uncomfortable and lonely. She, too, said nothing, wondering where the rest of the family had got to.

Presently a shrill voice called to Sarah from upstairs to fetch some fresh linen, and she rose quickly to obey. Micki was left to finish her hearty meal alone. Feeling much easier now that Sarah had gone, she cleaned her plate with enthusiasm. The maid came in to clear away the dishes; and at a loss as to what to do with herself, Micki began to wander about the dining room. Spotting an untouched morning newspaper on the sideboard, she glanced at it curiously. The paper felt very odd for a newspaper. The letters at the top were strangely complicated and hard to read, so that she could barely make out the name *The Morning Gazette*. Then Micki gasped.

The date on the paper read "April 19, 1891." The day was correct. It was the rest that was all wrong. The year was just over one hundred years ago! Micki's head spun. She felt almost sick with helplessness and had to fight hard to keep from panicking.

But she had little time to dwell on her situation, for the next moment a tall, fair-haired woman entered the room, leading a little girl by the hand. Her face was carefully powdered, but Micki could see from her red-rimmed eyes that she had been crying.

"Michelle, do forgive us for abandoning you. I'm your aunt Lydia, and this is Lizzie." Lizzie clung shyly to her mother's long skirts, peeping around at Micki with obvious curiosity. She reminded Micki of Jenny a few years ago.

"Goodness," Aunt Lydia exclaimed, peering closely at Micki. "Now that I've had a good look at you, I see you've grown into the image of your father. A DeSilver through and through!"

Micki was too taken aback to reply. DeSilver! It seemed too close to her own name to be a coincidence. And apparently she looked like Michelle's father as well.

"Sarah informs me she has told you about Gregory," said Aunt Lydia, lowering her voice slightly. "I'm sure you can see that she's terribly upset about her brother, as are we all. . . ." She trailed off and looked about her with a confused expression.

"He's not going to die, is he?" Micki blurted out

before she knew what she was saying.

These were the first words she had spoken to Aunt Lydia, and she realized, too late, how inappropriate they must sound coming from a stranger. But oddly enough she felt somehow bound up in the unfortunate accident of this boy she had never seen. After all, in a way she had been there when it happened. She could not think why, but Gregory's fate seemed of utmost importance to her.

"Let us pray to God not, Michelle," replied Aunt Lydia in the kind of voice that adults use when they are trying hard to hide what they are really feeling.

"Come, let me show you around the house, and perhaps we can find the rest of the family." Aunt Lydia led Micki out of the dining room and began giving her a guided tour. The rooms seemed to go on and on. There was obviously plenty of space for everyone, even with such a large family.

"Why does Sarah have to share her room with everyone else when they could have rooms of their own to play in?" Micki asked timidly, once they had passed through the final chambers on the second floor.

Aunt Lydia stopped short for a moment, but then smiled.

"Oh, has our Sarah complained to you already about that old family quarrel?" she said laughing.

"It so happens that it was part of the bargain for Sarah getting the attic room. All the children wanted it, so we were forced to compromise. But Sarah never lets anyone forget that it's really her room."

"What are you saying about me, Mama?" It was Sarah, who had just entered the room behind them carrying a bundle of linen from the sickroom.

"Michelle tells me you've already been bewailing how you're forced to share your room with your brothers and sisters. Really, Sarah, is that necessary?" said her mother with affectionate disapproval.

Micki felt Sarah's eyes turn toward her with hostility.

"No, I—" Micki faltered

"That's a lie, Mama! I never said any such thing!"

"Sarah, please! Michelle is a guest in this house. I will *not* have you speak to her in this fashion!"

Sarah clenched her fists in exasperation. Her eyes flashed with anger, and Micki squirmed beneath her gaze. Once more she tried to defend herself.

"I didn't mean—"

But Sarah had stormed out of the room.

Micki stood outside the huge stone house, staring up at the pattern of windows that dotted every floor until they converged in the oval-shaped glass beneath the attic eave. The house looked very imposing now that it was life-size, but there was no doubt that it was an exact duplicate of the doll-house Micki had seen in the museum the day before. Even the windowboxes and flowers were the same.

She was alone again. Aunt Lydia had gone back to tend to Gregory, taking Lizzie with her. Sarah had not reappeared, and Micki didn't dare seek her out.

She felt miserable and confused. How could she explain to Sarah about overhearing her conversation yesterday? Sarah would never believe her. Here she was, her first day in this house, and Sarah already hated her. And she would probably go on hating her, thinking that those rumors about her mean, sniveling cousin Michelle had been true all along. Try as she might, Micki could think of no way out of her predicament.

Already two strange things were happening to Micki. First, she was thinking and acting as if she were in this house to stay. Even if she wasn't the family's cousin Michelle, she might as well be— and Micki was beginning to think that perhaps she was after all.

Second, she was feeling something very new to

her. She was experiencing what it was like to be in someone else's shoes. She understood why Sarah was so angry. She would have felt the same way. And she liked Sarah all the more for standing up to her mother. It reminded her of herself, only Sarah was completely in the right. She wasn't so sure that was always the case with herself.

It was a beautiful day, and Micki felt comforted by the unseasonably warm April sunshine that poured down around her. It filtered through the leaves of the large maple tree that stood just to the side of the house and lit up the grass in patches of bright green. It was an unusual tree, with rough bark that looked almost silver. It looked very old and solemn. Micki drew closer and circled the sturdy trunk.

Then she glanced up and saw the huge gash. Where its lowest branch had once spread upward, strong enough to support three children, a broken limb hung, dangling listlessly. Shards of bark littered the ground.

Micki swallowed hard, her fingers tingling strangely. She looked quickly away, finding the sight almost physically painful. Instead, she gazed into the distance toward a faraway wooden fence that delineated the border of the DeSilver property.

Suddenly she caught sight of a small figure

creeping furtively along the far side of the railing. Micki could just make out the figure to be that of an old woman. She was carrying a large basket and was bent nearly double from its weight. Every now and then she would stop and look about her, as if to see whether she was alone on the road.

Micki watched her progress, fascinated. She seemed to be making her way slowly toward the house. For some reason Micki could not help thinking that there was something ominous in the old woman's approach. But before she drew close enough for Micki to be able to distinguish her features, two men appeared over the top of the hill along the road behind her.

In the blink of an eye the old woman had disappeared.

4

A Pack of Cousins

It was late afternoon when Micki returned from her wanderings about the DeSilver property. The house was surrounded by a broad grassy area that fed into a sweet-smelling evergreen forest filled with trails of soft pine needles. After Micki had rambled aimlessly through the woods for some time, she came upon a small lake hidden among a cluster of tall pine trees. As she scrambled over the slippery rocks at the lake's edge and waded through its chilly shallows in search of tadpoles,

Micki forgot her unhappiness and gave herself up to the glory of the bright April morning.

She wished she had on her jeans or some other outfit suitable for roaming through the countryside. As it was, her skirts were caked with mud within an hour. After that she stopped trying to hold them up as she traipsed about in solitary exploration.

Micki was not eager to go back to the house after her morning's encounters. Instead, once she had tired herself out with wading and running and climbing, she lay down on a bed of moss and pine needles that sloped down toward the lake. Then she promptly fell fast asleep. The sun had dipped far past the meridian when she awoke, but Micki had no idea what time it was, since she was not used to telling time except by the clock. Nevertheless, she thought she had best get back, in case the DeSilvers were looking for her.

Delicious smells emanated from the kitchen when she pushed open the front door. She had forgotten it was Sunday and that the family would probably be having some kind of midday meal. It was one of those things people used to do a long time ago.

She had been right about being missed. Aunt Lydia came briskly into the foyer as she stepped inside.

"My goodness, Michelle, where have you been? We'd begun to worry about you. Heavens, what a mess you are! You'd better hurry upstairs and wash and change your clothes. Dinner is nearly ready."

Micki looked down sheepishly at her sodden dress and, apologizing to her aunt, slunk upstairs to the attic room to change.

The door to the attic was closed. Micki hesitated, with her hand on the doorknob. Inside, she could hear the sound of hushed voices.

"No, we'll have to hold our meetings somewhere else from now on." It was Sarah speaking. "I'm not letting Michelle in on this. I know Gregory would have agreed."

"Sarah, why are you so unkind?" Micki recognized the voice of Sarah's older sister, Mary. "Michelle might see her while she's here. And we'd want to know about it. I'm sure Gregory would have wanted to tell her."

"No. I'm telling you, she's a nasty sneak. I wouldn't be surprised if she were spying on us now!" And before Micki knew what was happening, the door flew open and she stood face to face with her cousin Sarah.

"What did I tell you!" shouted Sarah in triumph.

Micki was horribly embarrassed.

"I haven't been spying, I swear!" she protested. "I just got here, and I heard you talking, so I didn't want to interrupt. I was getting ready to knock. *Really!* You've *got* to believe me!"

Sarah gazed at her with unmitigated hostility, but Mary seemed more inclined to be lenient.

"You look as if you've been dragged up from a river," she remarked, not unkindly. "By the way, I'm Mary."

"I know," said Micki. It was a moment before she realized that the reason she recognized Mary was through her eavesdropping the day before, but it was too late. "I mean I knew that Mary was the name of Sarah's older sister," she added lamely.

The three girls stood about for a minute in awkward silence. Micki turned beseechingly to Mary. The older girl, taking pity on her cousin, reached out a hand and said comfortingly, "Come, Michelle, let's get that filthy frock off of you so you can wash for dinner. We'll talk about all this later when some of us have had a chance to cool down," she added, glancing at her younger sister with mature disapproval.

It was Mary's kindness more than anything else that caused Micki to burst into the tears that had been wanting to come for two days now. Yesterday, when she was feeling so mean and angry, everyone had been trying to be pleasant to her and it had just made her angrier. Today, when she was trying hard to be nice and polite, it seemed as if she kept

46

being misunderstood. Sarah certainly took her to be just the opposite of nice.

"Please, please, it's not the way it seems—I can't explain—it's . . . I . . ." Her words were swallowed in a wave of uncontrollable weeping.

When her sobbing had finally subsided, and she had wiped her tear-stained face with the hem of her muddy dress, Micki appeared much the worse for her show of emotion.

"Michelle, now you could pass for a chimney sweep!" remarked Mary, unable to suppress a smile. Still, she held her cousin's hand, stroking it gently every now and again. For the first time that day Micki felt the warmth of another human being—not the distant politeness of Aunt Lydia, but the caring of someone who seemed to understand how miserable she was feeling. She smiled at Mary gratefully and felt a light pressure on her hand in return.

Sarah had retired to the other side of the room, where she was staring fixedly out the attic window. Apparently she had called a truce, for she said nothing as Mary went about the room gathering together fresh clothes for Micki. She even filled the washbasin, setting it out quietly on her cousin's dressing table. When she handed Micki a clean towel, their eyes met briefly, and Micki thought she could detect a slight softening in her gaze.

In any event, Micki felt distinctly better when the three of them finally made their way downstairs to dinner, where she was to meet the rest of the DeSilver clan.

When Micki followed her cousins into the dining room and saw a tall man standing by the sideboard talking to Aunt Lydia, she stopped in her tracks, her eyes wide with amazement. For a moment she thought she had returned to the present and that her father was standing before her. Surely anyone would take this man to be his brother if they were standing side by side. There was the same brown-black hair that had receded slightly, revealing a pronounced widow's peak; the same greeny-blue eyes flecked with hazel; and when he smiled at her in greeting, there was the same wide mouth twitching in amusement that looked ready to break into a full-blown laugh.

"So this is Michelle," the man said warmly, placing a large hand on each of her shoulders and gazing down at her face. He wore a long gray waistcoat, and a handsome gold watch chain looped out of his left-hand pocket.

"Your uncle Lucas has been out since early this morning, or you two would have met sooner," said Aunt Lydia. "And whom else haven't you met? Ah yes, Matthew," she said, gesturing to the little boy who stood behind the chair to her left. Matthew, however, seemed far more interested in reaching his fingers into the mint jelly than in making his cousin's acquaintance.

The family sat down to the table and Uncle Lucas began to say grace. Micki glanced about her curiously but, seeing all heads bowed, hastened to do the same.

"Lord, we give thanks for what you have set before us . . ." Uncle Lucas droned on for what seemed like a very long time. Micki began to fidget. Then his voice changed to one that sounded less sure and strong:

"And today, Lord, you have our special prayers, that our son and brother may be made well again, so that he may better serve your name . . ." he trailed off, and there was a moment of dead silence.

"Amen," Uncle Lucas concluded.

"Amen," repeated the family.

Micki felt a sudden flush. Her mouth was very dry and it was hard to swallow. There it was again, that strange, sick sensation she kept getting whenever she was reminded of Gregory. She tried to shake it off, but it seemed to hover there, beneath the surface of her consciousness.

"Yes," she whispered to herself, "please let him get well."

At first the dinner-table conversation was rather subdued as Uncle Lucas and Aunt Lydia exchanged a few remarks about household matters. It reminded Micki of one of the more boring dinners she might have had at home. Grownups often forgot there were other people around besides themselves.

As if reading her thoughts, Uncle Lucas turned to her and said, "So, Michelle, tell us about yourself. We know hardly anything about you!"

Micki nearly choked on her lamb, and a fit of coughing saved her from any immediate reply. But she was certain she was in for it. Then Lizzie saved the day. While her mother's attention was diverted, she apparently decided that her meat needed more gravy.

"Oh, Heavens!" exclaimed Aunt Lydia in dismay when she realized that Lizzie had managed to spill gravy all over the front of her dress, even though her mother had carefully tucked a cloth napkin into her pinafore before the meal began.

Next it was Matthew's turn. With no hesitation whatsoever, he stood up in his chair, reached unceremoniously across the table, and helped himself to a fistful of seconds on lamb. He was promptly given a firm smack on the bottom by his father. This led to a such a loud and tearful outburst that Micki was reminded of one of Jenny's performances when she was trying to get her big sister in trouble.

Amid the noise and confusion at the far end of the table the three older girls exchanged exasperated glances. For the first time Micki felt a faint bond with her cousins. Sarah rolled her eyes to the ceiling. Micki smiled back at her.

The maidservant came in and quietly beckoned to Aunt Lydia, who followed her out of the room. The family continued with their meal, though Matthew continued to sniffle dramatically into his napkin. After they had finished the roast lamb and potatoes, the fresh green peas, and the garden carrots in brown-sugar sauce, the table was cleared and the servant brought in a beautiful silver dish with the most sumptuous-looking dessert Micki had ever seen. Pieces of rich golden cake were laced together with a lemony yellow custard, and delicate rainbows of fruit in pink, orange, and yellow were sprinkled about the surface. The dish glistened in the dim light of the dying afternoon.

"What is it?" Micki murmured in wonder.

"Trifle, trifle, trifle!" shouted Lizzie, pounding her spoon on the table in excitement.

"Trifle is Lizzie's favorite dessert," commented Uncle Lucas dryly.

Micki couldn't help but agree. She had never tasted anything so good. The cake, the custard,

51

and the fruit all seemed to melt together into a single wonderful flavor that was nothing short of heaven. She thought she could have gone on eating it forever.

Just then, Aunt Lydia returned. Her eyes were moist with tears, but she was smiling.

"Gregory has regained consciousness. The doctor says he believes he is out of danger," she said quietly. Uncle Lucas rose from the table and put his arms around his wife. The children also pushed back their chairs and stood up. Mary hugged Sarah, Matthew began galloping wildly around the dining-room table, and Lizzie ran to her parents and clung to them for dear life. Micki alone remained seated, not knowing what to do or how to react. Nevertheless, she felt as though an enormous burden had been lifted.

"But he says it will be a long while before he is better," Aunt Lydia cautioned tremulously. "The fever is beginning to pass, but he is still extremely weak and needs a great deal of rest. Also, the doctor can't say wheth— when Gregory will be able to walk again, so we must all be very kind and very patient."

Everyone was quiet once Aunt Lydia had spoken these words. They seemed so final. But still, it felt as if the end were in sight, and it brought the family together. They all sat down again and finished their dessert. Under the circumstances, however, Micki thought it would be in poor taste to request thirds on trifle.

As the dinner dishes were being cleared away, Micki turned toward the large bay windows of the dining room with the thought of doing some more wandering about the grounds. But her face fell when she saw that the clear afternoon had turned ominous. Huge gray clouds had suddenly gathered on the horizon, and fat raindrops had already begun to splatter insistently against the windowpanes. She was reminded of yesterday's thwarted picnic, but it seemed a lifetime away.

"It looks as if you children will have to dream up some indoor activities this afternoon," commented Aunt Lydia. Mary and Sarah glanced at each other sourly. Evidently the prospect of coming up with "indoor activities" to entertain their cousin and young siblings was hardly appealing. But before either could express an opinion, Matthew began shouting excitedly, "Hide-and-go-seek! Sarah's It, Sarah's It!"

Sarah groaned. "Matthew, really! Mary and I are much too old to play that silly game. Why don't you, Lizzie, and Michelle play? Mary and I have to—"

"Sarah!" admonished Aunt Lydia severely. "Where are your manners? Michelle is your guest, and certainly if she's not too old to play, you aren't either. Please, darling," she added in a low voice, "just one or two games won't do you any harm. It would mean so much to Matthew—help take his mind off—"

"Of course, Mama," said Sarah, her manner changing completely. "Come along, Matthew. I'll be It. But mind you, no cheating this time. I don't expect you'll be slipping outside on a day like this, but just the same—anywhere outside the house is out of bounds. Last time we played, he hid in the barn," she said, turning to Micki in explanation. "It took us hours to find him. So then we had to lay down some rules: Anywhere inside the house is fair game. Anyone who goes outside has to forfeit and play It in the next round. All right, here I go. I'll count to fifty. One, two, three . . ."

Micki followed her cousins out of the room, but Matthew and Lizzie went tearing up the front stairs, and she felt too shy to follow Mary, who had turned left into the pantry. Feeling dreadfully awkward and alone in this big, unfamiliar house, she wandered through the back rooms on the main floor until Sarah's firm voice counting out the numbers had faded and become almost inaudible.

Micki tried to remember where she was from Aunt Lydia's tour, but it wasn't long before she was completely disoriented. Eventually she found herself in a large, dark room lit only by two orange-shaded lamps. The carved wood paneling was almost black, and shelf upon shelf of beautifully bound gold-lettered volumes reached up toward the ceiling. Micki's feet sank into a plush forest-green carpet, and she could smell the deep, rich scent of pipe tobacco and old leather.

"Oh my!" Micki breathed, and her fingers itched to pull down one of the lovely books that looked so inviting. If only she could just curl up in one of these armchairs and lose herself in a beautiful story about someone else, then she could forget about where she was and how she had got here. Perhaps a story about a poor orphan girl who finds out she has a family after all, a family of royal blood that is on the verge of dying out for lack of an heir. Micki was so taken with this idea that she began wandering dreamily about the room, embellishing her story with details and bits of conversation. When a deep male voice sounded not far off, she thought it was the father in her story.

"Do come into my study," the voice said. "I must have you look at some of the family papers. Much as I would like to avoid thinking the worst, I want everything to be in order in case he . . . well, in case I have to change my will."

"Certainly, sir," said Micki smiling. Then she shook herself, aghast. Why, this wasn't part of her story at all! It was the voice of Uncle Lucas, and he was heading straight for his study with an important guest!

Micki glanced hurriedly about the room for a means of escaping what would certainly be a very embarrassing situation. But the only way out except for the one now closed to her was through a small door in the corner of the room. Micki wrenched it open and, pulling it shut behind her, found she was not in another room but in what seemed like a small and musty closet.

"Now I've really landed in a mess," she thought, grimacing in the darkness. "I'm sure Sarah will never find me here, but how on earth will I ever get out—Uncle Lucas could be in there for hours, and everyone will be looking for me, and they'll think I've gone and cheated, and Sarah will hate me even more and . . . oh, I wish I could go home!"

As she said these words silently to herself, feeling once again on the verge of tears, Micki suddenly heard another voice. It was certainly not Uncle Lucas's voice, for the paneling of the closet door was so thick that it muffled all sound from without. Yet it was also so faint that Micki couldn't be sure where it was coming from or whether it was simply somewhere in the back of her head.

"Some of us do indeed get what we wish for,"

said the voice, and it seemed to hover for a moment, reverberating up toward the ceiling.

"This time I can't be dreaming," thought Micki, stepping backward, away from the haunting sound. Her foot struck against something, and she found herself tripping backward onto what seemed like a kind of shelf.

"Why, this isn't a closet at all, it's a staircase!" she exclaimed, forgetting her fright in the relief of finding a way out of her immediate dilemma. It was indeed a staircase, and now that her eyes were growing accustomed to the dim light, Micki could see that it was not as dark and airless as she had originally thought. In fact, the stair was lit from the top, where Micki could just make out a door opening onto the floor above.

Eagerly, she climbed the stairs, feeling her way with her fingers along the rough plaster walls. When she reached the top and pushed through the heavy wooden door, she found herself at the end of a long, narrow hallway that gave off onto a series of rooms on either side. From the room closest to her, an old servant emerged carrying something heavy on her arm. Her tiny bent form glided noiselessly down the long corridor toward another set of stairs at the far end of the house. For a moment Micki thought her eyes were playing tricks on her and the woman had actually faded into the wall itself.

"Where can she be?" said a voice rising from the front stairwell. It was Sarah. Micki was on the verge of calling out, "Here I am!" when she remembered she was supposed to be playing a game of hide-and-go-seek. She would certainly look very silly if after looking for her so long they found her wandering about aimlessly in the hallway. So she quickly ducked into the room from which she had just seen the maid emerge.

It was completely dark inside, and an unpleasant medicinal smell hung in the air. Micki could dimly identify the shapes of a bureau, a dressing table, and a large four-poster bed. It was not until she heard a faint groan and a rustling of sheets that she realized that she was not alone in the room. She drew closer to the huge bed and looked down. There, framed by airy heaps of white pillows, lay the pallid face of a boy some years older than herself. She knew at once that it could be none other than Gregory DeSilver.

5

Gregory

There was no one else in the room. The woman whom Micki had mistaken for one of the servants must have been the attending nurse gone to fetch something. She was certain to return momentarily. Micki turned quickly to go, but then hesitated. It had just occurred to her that if anyone were to see her leaving the sickroom, particularly Sarah, she would have to do some fast explaining.

Gregory moaned softly. His pale forehead was damp with sweat. He looked pathetically weak and almost bloodless. Suddenly he flung his arm across his face as if to fend off an imaginary blow. He began mumbling incoherently, rocking his head back and forth on the pillow. Micki drew closer, fascinated. Gradually, through his constant repetition, she began to make out some of what he was saying.

He seemed obsessed by the idea of trees and broken branches. "It'll snap in two, like that!" he kept muttering, gesturing vaguely with one hand.

He must be dreaming about his horrible accident, Micki thought. Suddenly Gregory sat up straight, his eyes wide and staring at something unseen in front of him. When he opened his mouth to speak, Micki was seized with horror. For the voice was not the voice of a boy. It was the voice of an old woman.

"Beware of that cousin, young man—she'll snap the DeSilvers in two like a branch of dry kindling!"

Then he screamed. Micki had never heard such a sound before. It hit her like a physical blow, and she had to reach out and grasp the nearby bedpost for support. It was as if someone had torn the scream from his throat.

"Too late!" came the terrible cry.

Before Micki could respond or call for help, Sarah had burst into the room.

"Oh my God, Gregory!" she shrieked, running to him with her arms outstretched. Then whirling around, she faced Michelle. "What are you doing in here? What have you done to him? Mama, Mama, come quickly—something's happened to Gregory!" she called desperately.

Micki had neither moved nor taken her eyes from Gregory's face. He was quiet now, but he was gripping his sister's hands as if she were connecting him with life itself. For the first time he seemed conscious of another person, and he stared at her with a pleading look in his eyes.

"Sarah, I saw her yesterday. She wanted to warn me against Cousin Michelle. But she's just come to me again. 'Too late—the deed is done,' she said. 'Now the branch must come to the tree or the tree will wither and die!' What did she mean, Sarah? What did she mean?" Gregory's eyes once again became clouded and began to wander about the room.

"Gregory!" shouted Sarah, shaking her brother so roughly that his head jerked back and forth, but it was useless. He no longer recognized her.

"You!" she flung at Micki. "Look what you've done!"

The room was now filled with people. Aunt Lydia had come running when she heard Sarah call, and the rest of the family followed soon after.

The nurse stood at the foot of the bed wringing her hands in dismay. She was a tall woman of middle age. Micki stared at her with a puzzled expression. This was certainly not the person she had seen leaving the room only moments ago.

"What happened to him?" demanded Aunt Lydia, glaring at the nurse. "Why was he left alone?"

"Madam, I only left at your own request when you came to relieve me," the woman replied.

"I? Why, I haven't been near this room for the past hour, Mrs. Cage."

The nurse stared at her. "But Madam, I heard you distinctly from where I was straightening up in the sitting room. You said you wished to sit with Mr. Gregory awhile alone. So I toddled off to the kitchen for a quick cup of tea."

"Really, Mrs. Cage, I think it's more than tea you've been drinking. I tell you, I've been in the drawing room going over the accounts since we finished dinner."

The nurse shook her head in disbelief.

Aunt Lydia drew up a chair next to her son's bed and felt his forehead anxiously.

"Heavens, he's burning up! Mrs. Cage, quick, have someone fetch Dr. Bain immediately. Gregory has taken a terrible turn for the worse."

Micki watched this exchange in silence. She felt

sorry for the nurse, who appeared dreadfully upset at having her credibility called into question. She wondered whether she ought to speak up and say she had seen someone leaving Gregory's room a little while ago. But she was terrified of bringing attention to herself and being forced to give an explanation of her own. She had nearly forgotten that she had only wandered into the sickroom by accident.

It was not long before the doctor was ushered into the room by Mrs. Cage. He had lost no time in answering her urgent summons, and he rushed in, his hat and dripping umbrella still in his hands.

Dr. Bain was a small man with a round, pink face and sympathetic blue eyes. Sparse wisps of snow-white hair sprang out in all directions around his smooth, otherwise bald pate. A pair of tiny gold spectacles perched at the tip of his rather bulbous nose, threatening to slip off at any moment. He carried a huge black bag that was far too big for him, and he had to fairly hoist it up onto the night-stand next to the bed. He glanced around at the crowded room with mild disapproval.

"Tut, tut! This is a sickroom, not a circus!" he admonished, but not unkindly. At a gesture from Aunt Lydia, Mary took Lizzie and Matthew each firmly by the hand and escorted them out of the room under violent protest. As no one else made a move to leave, the doctor turned to his patient without further comment and began pulling various instruments and bottled liquids out of his bottomless bag.

Gregory was deeply unconscious and responded to none of the doctor's proddings and pokings. The doctor clicked his tongue now and then in concern until he had completed his examination.

"The boy seems to have received some kind of emotional shock since I last saw him," he said, shaking his head gravely when he had finished. "I believe it must be that, rather than any physical development, that is responsible for this drastic reversal. I'm afraid, Mrs. DeSilver, that for the moment there is nothing more I can do except continue his current treatment. We must watch and wait."

Aunt Lydia bit her lower lip to keep it from trembling.

"Please don't misunderstand me," he added quickly, noticing her distress. "We are by no means to lose hope. Your son's condition may very well be only temporary. Nevertheless, I would give a great deal to learn what it was that shocked him into this state."

"Why don't you ask Michelle?" demanded Sarah, glaring at her cousin fiercely. "She was in the room when Gregory started screaming."

All eyes turned expectantly to Micki. She felt her face flush hot with embarrassment. She was barely able to string together the words of a response.

"I didn't know this was his room," she mumbled. "It wasn't me! I didn't do anything, I swear! It was someone else!" she cried, looking desperately from one blank face to the other.

"No one has accused you of anything, Michelle," said Aunt Lydia quietly. But Micki barely heard her. In tears of frustration, she ran from the room.

Micki headed straight for the attic. After the day's events, she dreaded having to share this room with Sarah. It was apparent that she had lost any headway she might have made earlier in befriending her. Gregory's strange and ominous words about their terrible cousin Michelle had obviously sealed her fate. Unless Micki could convince her otherwise—that *she* was not this evil person—from now on Sarah would consider her an enemy. She would also hold her responsible for Gregory's relapse.

While the attic room was certainly unwelcoming, Micki could think of nowhere else to go. At least for the moment it would be unoccupied. Micki threw herself onto her bed and buried her face in the pillow. She lay there for some time, her eyes screwed tightly shut. Perhaps, she thought fervently, if she really concentrated, she could transport herself back home to her own room and her own bed. But try as she would, she only succeeded in giving herself a headache.

She sat up when she heard low voices on the stair.

"Of course I would never believe *Michelle* saying it was someone else." The voice was Sarah's. "But I can't stop thinking about what Gregory told me right before he ... he ..." She wasn't able to finish.

"What was it?" It was Mary.

"He said, 'She's just come to me again.'"

"Do you think it was *she* who frightened him, then? But how is that possible? How could she have got into his room, or into the house for that matter?"

"Shhh," hissed Sarah.

The sisters had reached the top of the stairs, and their voices dropped to a barely audible whisper. Micki watched them as they entered the room, Sarah's face an uncommunicative mask. Mary, too, was quiet.

"How is he?" asked Micki, looking away.

"Why should you care?" snapped Sarah.

"Sarah!" exclaimed Mary, shocked at her sister's

vehemence. "He's much the same," she said, turning to Micki. "Dr. Bain says he'll return in the morning, and perhaps then he'll have a better idea of how serious Gregory's condition is."

Micki stood up and walked to the window. The rain had not let up. It lashed angrily at the dark pane, and the wind whistled like the ceaseless refrain of a chorus, sending cold gusts of air through the cracks in the wood. She pressed her nose against the glass and watched as her hot breath made a ragged circle of steam that quickly faded inward when she pulled away.

She turned to face her cousins.

"I know you don't believe me, but there *was* someone in Gregory's room before me," she said urgently.

"Who?" asked Mary.

"I don't *know* who," replied Micki. "All I know is that I saw someone come out of the room before I went in. When I figured out it was Gregory's room I was in, I thought it must have been the nurse leaving to take something downstairs. But it wasn't. She was much too small. Tiny, in fact. And she looked like she was carrying something heavy."

Mary and Sarah exchanged glances.

"It *was* her," they breathed simultaneously.

"But how could she have gotten into the house

67

with no one seeing?" asked Mary excitedly.

"You remember the times we each saw her," replied Sarah. "She seemed to simply *appear*. We hadn't seen her just the moment before, and then there she was."

"Or there she wasn't," put in Micki. "The person I saw was headed for the front stairs as Sarah was coming up. But I never actually saw her reach them. I know it sounds strange, but it almost looked like she faded into the wall."

"I certainly saw no one," said Sarah.

"But that's just it!" cried Mary. "Don't you remember what Gregory said just the other day? He figured she's only seen when she wants to be seen."

Suddenly Micki remembered something: the old woman she had spotted making her way toward the house yesterday morning. She felt sure it was the same person. Eagerly she described the incident to her cousins.

The two sisters listened attentively to Micki's story. Without words they seemed to have agreed that the situation was too grave to keep their cousin in the dark any longer. Together they related how they had first become aware of the mysterious old woman. About a month ago, she had appeared at the house, apparently selling eggs from one of the nearby farms. No one was at home but Gregory, Sarah, and the servants. The two had been climbing in the large maple tree outside the house, and they had spied the woman making her way to the servants' entrance with her enormous basket. When she had left, instead of taking the main road by the side of the house, she had simply disappeared into the woods. Later the cook had commented that it was strange the woman had never called at the house before.

On the second occasion, which took place only a few days later, it was Matthew and Mary who saw her. They were returning from a visit to a neighbor, walking quite slowly along the main road, when they suddenly overtook the woman headed in the same direction toward their house. She turned to greet them almost as if she were expecting them. The woman seemed to know exactly who they were and made a particular point of inquiring after their brother. She said she hoped to see him one day soon—why, they could not imagine. Then she had turned off at the next side road and quickly disappeared.

After that there was no further sign of her for some time. But just last week, Gregory saw her again from his perch in the maple tree. The gardener was working nearby, but his back was turned the other way. Gregory said the woman emerged from the woods and began to sniff the air like a fox or a rabbit in search of something. Then, as if deciding the winds were not in her favor, she returned as quickly as she had come.

The four older children began to talk frequently about the old woman among themselves. They held secret meetings in Sarah's attic room during which they went over and over the details of their most recent sighting and speculated as to when she might appear again. There was something about her that had made a deep impression on all four children—even Matthew, who was generally oblivious to these things.

Who was she? Why was she so interested in Gregory? Answers to these questions seemed more imperative than ever, for it now appeared certain that Gregory had seen the woman not long before his accident—in fact, they explained to Micki, he had called a meeting for that very afternoon to discuss his latest discovery. Whatever it was, it must have been on his mind when he fell, for it obviously continued to obsess him.

Sarah began to pace the room restlessly, her brows knit in concentration.

"We must have a plan," said Mary. "It's the only way we can help Gregory. Somehow we must find out what she did to him—what she said to cause him to take on so."

A plan, Micki thought. A plan that includes me.

She was so delighted that her cousins were finally accepting her that nothing else seemed to matter—not even the reason such a plan was needed in the first place. She would do anything, even face the dreadful old woman alone, if only they would stop misunderstanding her.

Then Micki turned and saw the wooden look on Sarah's face. Her cousin stood stockstill in the middle of the room. It was as if she'd caught herself just in time.

"Mary, I think you're forgetting something." Her voice was very quiet. "Gregory spoke to me before he went unconscious again. He *told* me what the woman said. And it had to do with *you!*" Her eyes flashed accusingly at Micki. "So what I want to know is how does she know who you are, and why has she been warning Gregory against you?"

The quiet in the room was so complete that Micki could almost hear the beating of her heart. But she could only stare mutely at her cousins, as at a loss for an explanation as they.

6

Lessons

The following day brought no improvement in either the weather or Gregory's condition. True to his word, early that morning Dr. Bain braved the pouring rain to call on his patient. But he had no good news to report except that there was no change for the worse.

Uncle Lucas had left the house shortly after the doctor's visit, but the rest of the family breakfasted together. A heavy silence reigned throughout most of the meal. Even Matthew and Lizzie said very little and engaged in none of the antics of the afternoon before.

While the dishes were being cleared, Aunt Lydia, who had hardly touched her food, said gravely to her two elder daughters, "I think today we should busy ourselves with quieter activities. After your morning lessons you had best get on with some needlework."

Micki's heart sank. Lessons and *needlework*! This was supposed to be her holiday! Once again she thought of home with a sharp pang. For a moment she had hopes that as a guest in the house she would be spared these unpleasant occupations, but unfortunately Aunt Lydia had other things in mind for her.

"Michelle, since you will probably be with us for some time, I think perhaps you might as well join Sarah and Mary with their instruction," she said firmly. "Miss Collins will be here in half an hour. Sarah will show you to the music room in case you've forgotten where it is."

When Aunt Lydia had risen from the table, Sarah glanced at Micki with frank hostility. There had been little change in her attitude since yesterday evening.

"She seems to know where most of the other rooms in the house are," she muttered unkindly under her breath so that her mother couldn't hear. Mary, however, lowered her brows in disapproval.

"Sarah has some tidying up to do in her room, Mother. I'd be happy to take Michelle in when I go," she said. Sarah shrugged her shoulders indifferently but looked slightly ashamed.

The music room was situated in the east wing of the house, and the large bay windows on two sides of the room were purposely designed to admit the morning light. On a sunny day, the atmosphere would have been bright and cheerful. Today, however, the expanse of glass made one acutely aware of the grim weather, and the room felt cold and depressing.

A medium-sized piano stood on very thin legs in the center of the room, and next to it a beautiful harp carved out of a deep reddish wood. Seated at the harp was a sallow young woman wearing a plain brown dress. She was busy plucking at the instrument and adjusting the strings as she listened carefully to each note. The woman looked up smiling. Her teeth were rather crooked, and she closed her lips down over them as if realizing they were exposed. She had very pale, watery-blue eyes.

"Good morning, girls," she said. "Ah, I see you have brought your cousin Michelle. Michelle, I'm Miss Collins, your instructress. I look forward to our work together. I presume your previous studies will allow you to keep up with our curriculum. However, we shall see. Today I believe we'll start with our music lessons, and then see how you've come along with your French grammar. Mary, why don't you begin?"

Mary seated herself obediently beside the harp, arranged her music in front of her, and proceeded to pluck out a very delicate tune. Once she made a mistake and had to go back and find her place in the piece, but otherwise she seemed to play with competence. To Micki, however, the music was dull, and she found herself squirming the way she did at school when they brought in people from the orchestra and made the class sit and listen attentively. The teachers called this activity "music appreciation," but Micki never felt very appreciative.

When Mary was finally done, Miss Collins smiled at her with approval.

"You're coming along quite nicely, Mary. Just remember that your hands must *float* across the strings, like so," she said demonstrating. "Now Sarah, it's your turn. Have you brought the sonata I left you to practice last week?"

Sarah, who was already seated at the piano, ignored her teacher's question and instead began to play. At first the music sounded like any basic exercise that a pupil might play to warm up at the beginning of a lesson. But suddenly, with no warning, Sarah launched into a piece of such complexity and beauty that Micki was amazed. Her small fingers flew across the keyboard, now gentle, now pounding the keys with a passion. Her eyes were closed and little beads of perspiration had begun to stand out on her forehead. She was completely engrossed in her playing. Micki hardly dared to breathe just watching her.

"Sarah, please, *please!*" Miss Collins had placed her hands over her pupil's so that the music ceased. "Such violence, Sarah, really. How many times must I tell you that your playing is positively unladylike? Now begin again."

"Oh no!" Micki cried out in Sarah's defense. "I thought it was wonderful! I could never play like that."

Sarah flushed. For the first time she looked at her cousin with something like grateful acknowledgment.

"Nonsense, Michelle. I'm sure you play very well," replied Miss Collins, who managed to smile and look annoyed at the same time. "Why don't you come and show us?" she added gesturing to the piano seat.

"Oh no! I can't play. All I know is 'Heart and Soul.'"

Miss Collins looked puzzled. "Well, come along then."

"Who's going to play the other part?"

"Michelle, I haven't the slightest idea what you're talking about. Do sit down."

Micki took her seat reluctantly at the piano as Sarah shifted over to one end of the bench. She fingered the keyboard tentatively, trying to remember how the song went. Then the rhythmic, simple notes came to her and she began jerkily to play. Gradually she relaxed and started to enjoy herself. But when she looked up at the end of the piece, Micki was startled to see Miss Collins and Mary gazing at her aghast. Sarah sat facing her with one hand clapped over her mouth to stifle a giggle, her blue eyes sparkling merrily.

"Michelle, who on earth taught you that dreadful song?" gasped Miss Collins.

"I like it," said Sarah, flashing her instructor an impish grin.

"Would you like to learn the other part?" asked Micki shyly.

Sarah smiled. "Very much."

But before the two cousins could begin, Miss Collins stopped them with a disapproving look.

"Some other time perhaps, girls. For the moment, I think we'll leave the music and move on to French." She motioned them to a large table at the opposite end of the room, on which was stacked a collection of primers and notebooks. A neat line of fountain pens protruded from smooth, round inkwells.

"Now I trust you remember that last week we reviewed the subjunctive. Mary, please start us off by conjugating the verb 'connaître.'"

"Connaître. To know or be acquainted with," began Mary dutifully. "The subjunctive form: que je connaisse, que tu connaisses . . ." The strange words rolled easily off her tongue.

Now Micki felt truly out of her depth. She knew no French whatsoever—in her class at school they were learning Spanish. And she certainly had no idea what the words "conjugate" or "subjunctive" meant. When her turn came to recite an exercise, she had no alternative but to confess her ignorance.

"You have no French?" exclaimed Miss Collins. She seemed extremely put out. "Why, you ignorant girl, where *have* you been brought up? Perhaps you'd like to tell us what exactly you *do* know," she added, making little attempt to disguise the sarcasm in her voice.

Micki thought for a moment. "I can count to ten in base four," she responded brightly. "And I'm starting to learn algebra." Math was Micki's favorite subject in school, and she was in the advanced class.

"Algebra," sniffed Miss Collins, "is hardly a

suitable subject for a young lady. You'll certainly not find *me* filling your head with any such useless nonsense. I'm afraid you've a great deal to learn, Michelle."

For the remainder of their lessons, Micki tried to be as unobtrusive as possible. She listened as her cousins passed obediently from one subject to the other, translating passages from French to English and back again, making sketches, called still lives, from groups of objects assembled by their teacher, and reciting endlessly boring lines of poetry about spring blossoms and nightingales. It was all Micki could do to keep from falling asleep in her chair. She tried pinching herself once or twice, but she couldn't feel anything through all her layers of pinafores and petticoats.

Miss Collins made no further attempt to involve Micki in the lessons, saying condescendingly that she would have to speak to Mrs. DeSilver later about arranging for special "remedial" instruction. Mary looked at her pityingly when Miss Collins said this, but Sarah flashed her a secret smile.

Finally the lessons were over, and after a light midday meal—nothing like the sumptuous repast they had enjoyed on Sunday—Aunt Lydia reminded the girls of their scheduled afternoon's activity. She led them into the sitting room and brought out two huge baskets filled with assorted yarns and fabrics. Mary and Sarah selected out their respective pieces of work and carried them to their seats. A cozy fire had been lit in the grate, and Micki watched the hot tongues of flame lick their way along the dry logs and kindling. After her rather humiliating morning, she was more than content to sit and do nothing. But, once again, her aunt had other plans in mind for her.

"Michelle, you must begin a project since you seem to have brought none with you," said Aunt Lydia. "How about taking over this pillow embroidery that Sarah began and never finished," she suggested, handing Micki a wooden hoop clamped tightly over a piece of cloth. Sketched lightly on the material was an intricate floral pattern that had been partially filled in with tiny, painstaking stitches.

Micki looked around her at the others. They had already settled comfortably into their work, Sarah to her right and Mary and Aunt Lydia across from her. Each seemed completely absorbed. Helplessly, she examined the bits of colored thread that hung in a tangled web from beneath her piece of handiwork. One of the threads was attached to a small snub-nosed needle. She poked it dubiously through the cloth and pulled it through with a jerk. The thread snapped from the force of her effort, and the needle went flying, landing squarely in the fireplace and disappearing among the glowing embers.

"Oh dear!" she exclaimed in embarrassment at her clumsiness.

Aunt Lydia glanced up with a questioning look.

"I seem to have lost my needle," said Micki sheepishly. Aunt Lydia rummaged through her workbasket and handed her niece another needle. Then she watched in disbelief as Micki tried fruitlessly to thread it.

"Michelle, anyone would think you'd never done a stitch of embroidery in your life," she admonished.

"Well, as a matter of fact, I haven't," Micki admitted.

"Honestly! I thought Miss Collins was exaggerating when she told me you were shockingly untutored, but now I'm beginning to believe she was right," said her aunt. "What *have* they been teaching you all these years?"

Remembering how Miss Collins had reacted when she answered this question, Micki felt it best to say nothing. Instead she hung her head in shame, and Aunt Lydia instantly softened and took pity on her.

"Well it's not your fault, poor child," she said kindly. "But now that you've come to stay with us, we'll have to make up for lost time. I'll take things in hand myself, and I'm sure we'll see you an expert with the needle before very long. Also, if I'm not mistaken," she added, eyeing her younger daughter, who was ripping out a row of imperfect stitches, "Sarah could use a little extra instruction herself."

"Oh thank you, Aunt Lydia," said Micki, beaming. She surprised herself. Learning how to sew was certainly not a prospect to be relished. But she was so grateful for Aunt Lydia's kindness and interest that she thought even needlework might be endured.

That night, as Micki lay in bed staring up at the sloping attic roof, a thought occurred to her. Just a few days ago, when she was at home with her parents and sister, she couldn't stand their concern. All she wanted was to be left alone. Since then, she had done a complete about-face. Now she craved attention, as long as it was kind. She smiled to herself. "Maybe that's what they call 'learning one's lesson,'" she thought wryly, as she drifted off to sleep.

It seemed like only seconds had passed when she heard a voice.

"Michelle! Michelle! Wake up!" Sarah was standing over her, shaking her roughly.

"What is it? What's wrong?" she asked, sitting up with a start.

"You were talking in your sleep," said Sarah. "It sounded as if you were having a terrible dream. You were speaking quite loudly. It woke me up."

"What was I saying?" She frequently remembered her dreams, but this one had fled like a dissipating cloud.

"All I could make out was something about dry kindling." Dry kindling. Micki's head began to clear.

"Gregory. Gregory's dream," she said softly. Sarah had lit the candle next to their bed, and her eyes flickered in its pale light. She held it up to Micki's face.

"What dream, Michelle?"

"Today . . . yesterday . . . when I was in there alone . . ." Micki faltered. It was so difficult to talk about it, knowing what Sarah must be thinking.

"Yes?" prompted Sarah eagerly.

"Well, he kept muttering in his sleep about trees and branches. At first I thought he was dreaming about his terrible fall from the tree, but then he said something else." Micki paused again. "You have to promise not to hate me if I tell you, Sarah."

Sarah's eyes narrowed. "Very well."

"He said 'Beware of that cousin—she'll snap the DeSilvers in two like a branch of dry kindling!'"

Micki watched Sarah closely to see whether she could gauge her reaction. But her face was impassive.

"Sarah, you must believe me—I'm not who you think I am."

"Who are you then?" asked Sarah. She sounded just slightly sarcastic.

"You wouldn't believe me if I tried to explain," replied Micki weakly. "But I'm telling you, there's something strange and horrible going on. And I think it has to do with that old woman. Because when Gregory said that... that... thing, it wasn't his voice. It was *her* voice, I'm sure of it. It was like she had somehow got *inside* of him."

Sarah's face was pale. "Poor Mrs. Cage," she murmured. "Mother discharged her for shirking her duty, but if I'm not mistaken, she must have been terribly misjudged."

Micki nodded slowly in agreement. The nurse had been sent packing for fabricating stories to cover up her neglectful behavior. But if that mysterious and frightening old woman had been able to put some kind of spell on Gregory, could she not have done the same to Mrs. Cage? Perhaps what the unfortunate nurse had heard coming from the adjacent bedroom was actually a very clever imitation of Aunt Lydia's voice asking her for a few minutes alone with her son.

Both girls were silent for a moment. "It doesn't make any sense," said Sarah finally.

"What doesn't?"

"Why? Why would that woman want to hurt Gregory?"

"Why would I?" countered Micki.

"I think she came in specifically to tell Gregory something," said Sarah, ignoring Micki's remark. "Do you remember what he said to me when he knew who I was?"

"Yes."

"He'd been given a message," Sarah continued, as if in a trance. "By her: 'Now the branch must come to the tree or the tree will wither and die.' I can't make it out, but I have this dreadful feeling that the tree doesn't actually mean a tree, but a person."

Suddenly the air in the attic room felt close and oppressive. Micki's palms had begun to sweat, and she rubbed them on her pillow. The candle sputtered violently, even though there was not the slightest breeze.

"Michelle, I'm so dreadfully afraid. Afraid that woman was telling Gregory that he's going to die."

Micki couldn't think of a single word to comfort her cousin, she was so convinced that Sarah was right. It was some time before either of them was able to fall asleep, and their slumber was fitful at best.

7

Mirrors in the Stone

It was not long before Micki realized that learning how to be a "young lady" was a full-time occupation. What one did once this exalted position had been achieved she wasn't sure, but she was given little time to speculate.

Aunt Lydia had very much "taken things in hand," and hardly a day passed when Micki was not subject to her unswerving attention as she learned to ply a needle. While at first she spent more time ripping out her work than executing it, within a week her aunt had taught her the rudiments of embroidery as well as several other forms of needlecraft.

Last week Micki had begun something called a "sampler," a piece of heavy cloth, rather like fine burlap, onto which she had to stitch individual letters that formed words, and eventually phrases. Micki remembered seeing something like this in a museum that her mother had taken her to last year. Aunt Lydia, as a gesture of encouragement, was allowing her to choose her own phrase for the sampler. But first she had to complete every letter of the alphabet perfectly. Micki had been very diligent, and much to Aunt Lydia's surprise and delight, she was already up to the letter W.

Micki's instruction under Miss Collins was less successful. There were some things, such as French grammar, that she picked up quite quickly and easily. However, other subjects—poetry, for example—frankly bored her, and she made little progress. Miss Collins proved an impatient instructor, and threw up her hands in disgust whenever Micki failed to properly recite the lines assigned to her.

Fortunately for Micki, she was not Miss Collins' only neglectful pupil. Sarah, too, had no patience for memorization and was more vocal about her distaste for it than Micki. More than once Miss

Collins was forced to complain to Aunt Lydia about Sarah's impudence, which apparently had become worse since her cousin's arrival. A week spent together under Miss Collins' severe and watchful eye did more to break through Sarah's coolness and create a bond between the two cousins than anything Micki could have done or said.

Just under two weeks had passed since Micki had arrived in the DeSilver household, and she was beginning to wonder whether she was there for good. She tried to imagine what her parents and Jenny must be thinking now that she'd been gone for so long.

Maybe they don't miss me at all, she thought unhappily. Micki decided not to think about it.

Fortunately, this morning the weather had finally changed, allowing her to escape her rigorous schedule of instruction for a few blissful hours out of doors. She left the house quite early, while Sarah was still asleep. At first Micki was tempted to wake her cousin and ask her to come for a morning walk in the woods, but she changed her mind and decided that it was probably best if she went alone.

It was a mild day, and the air was rich with the smell of the damp earth releasing its moisture into the sunlight. The sky was clear blue, nearly cloudless, and the light breeze blowing through the trees made their branches look like arms beckoning her into the woods.

She trudged off eagerly. Since realizing that she had no choice but to be trussed up in the miserable clothing of the nineteenth century, Micki had become much more adept at handling her long skirts and moved with comparative freedom across the wide meadow toward the woods.

Her walk took her back to the little lake where she had played so happily the afternoon of her first day with the DeSilvers. Today she was not in the mood to go hunting for tadpoles. Still, there was something about this shady glen and its view of the calm blue-green water that Micki found comforting.

Micki seated herself against a large pine tree. Her face was toward the early-morning sun, and behind her the woods whispered gently. It felt good to get away. While she was starting to feel more at ease in the DeSilver household, there remained that sense of being an outsider, even with Sarah. It was true that her cousin had begun to treat her more kindly and spoke to her openly about her fears for her brother. But the precarious state of Gregory's health seemed to create a barrier between Micki and the entire family.

Micki kept hoping that the situation would be

only temporary, but the news of two nights ago put an end to her hopes. Dr. Bain had paid his daily visit just before the evening meal. He was closeted with Aunt Lydia and Uncle Lucas for a long while after examining Gregory, so the children knew things must be serious. But they didn't expect to be told anything.

They were wrong. Directly after dinner, Uncle Lucas looked around the table and said quietly, "Children, your mother and I feel it isn't right to keep this from you. The doctor has informed us that he believes Gregory's relapse is irreversible. Only a miracle can keep him with us now."

After the news had sunk in, Sarah ran sobbing to her room, and Micki was too uncomfortable to go anywhere near her until it was time for bed. When she finally went upstairs, Sarah was already in bed with the light out and a pillow clasped over her head. The next day she was quiet and subdued, almost resigned. Nevertheless, Micki was ill at ease. She felt as if Sarah were watching her again, even though she was outwardly polite.

Micki stirred the pine needles with her hand. Throughout the past two weeks, Gregory's relapse had never ceased to trouble her, especially the connection it appeared to have with herself. That Gregory was almost definitely going to die seemed to her impossible. How was it the doctor could do nothing for him?

"It's simply not fair!" she said angrily. "They can't let him die!"

Suddenly she heard a faint rustling of leaves, like a small animal scrabbling in the undergrowth. She turned toward the noise and then sharply drew in her breath. Where before there had been nothing but the shadows of tree branches playing in the sunlight, there now stood the tiny figure of an old woman. She was bent over by the weight of a huge and heavily laden basket. Micki had no doubt who the woman was.

"Ah, if it isn't the sour little chicken, having a taste of her own medicine." The old woman chuckled merrily as if expressing her appreciation for an inside joke.

For a moment Micki simply stared. Then, without thinking, she blurted out: "It was you, wasn't it? It was you who was in Gregory's room that day. When you left he had a relapse, and now he's going to die. You've killed him!"

"I, chicken? No, not I. I only provide the warnings. Never the deeds." The woman peered at Micki closely. The dark brown eyes seemed to look deep within her, making her squirm with discomfort. It was a look Micki was sure she had seen somewhere before.

"It was fear of his evil cousin that gave the boy his fatal blow, not I," said the woman.

"But they all think that's me!"

"And so they should."

"But it's not me! I'm not their horrible cousin. I've done nothing to hurt Gregory and I don't plan to!"

"Ah, but the deed's already done, chicken."

"What do you mean?"

"Sometimes a wish can kill," replied the woman. And stretching out her free hand, she opened her leathery palm wide and began to chant in a sing-song voice:

"The branch once turned to the trunk and said,
'Though it's not my wish to see you dead,
I'd so much rather we severed ties.'
But in snapping free the whole tree dies.

"It's up to you now, little Micki Silver," she said. "Only you can undo and unsay the evil thing. But remember, if you fail, you might as well never have existed. In fact, you won't have existed."

"Won't have existed?" repeated Micki, thoroughly puzzled. The woman's manner of speaking was making her head spin.

Without taking her eyes from Micki's face, the old woman reached into her basket and drew out a round object the size of her hand. In a flash she tossed it in Micki's direction, and it landed beside her with a heavy thud. Micki picked it up. It was a smooth, beautiful, rose-colored stone, speckled and shaped like a giant hen's egg.

"Which came first, the chicken or the egg?" the old woman cackled.

"Oh please!" Micki whimpered. "Please, I don't understand!"

"Don't you? Perhaps you should go to the source. Branch to the trunk. Ask your father, chicken, ask your father. And remember, nothing is cast in stone!"

A faint breeze caused the tree branches to cast a deep shadow over the spot where the old woman was standing. For a moment the sunlight filtering through the pine needles imposed a mosaic pattern over her gnarled face and figure. Then the pattern cracked and dissolved, and Micki was left staring at an empty space in front of her.

When she looked down at the beautiful stone in her lap, she was surprised to see that it had split in two. She took one half in each hand and held them in front of her. The egg had cracked evenly down the center—the oval pieces were identical in size. While the round, smooth, speckled outside of the egg was a delicate rose color, the flat side where the crack had occurred was a pale whitish gray.

As Micki gazed first at one half of the egg, then at the other, the oddest thing happened. It made her forget the mysterious old woman and her equally mysterious disappearance. Because all of a sudden the surface of half the egg started to move. The rough ridges became little silvery waves that rippled gently back and forth. For some time this movement continued, and Micki felt so soothed by it that she began to feel drowsy. Then, as if the rippling had been caused by a breeze that ceased to blow, the waves stopped, and the surfaces became smooth as glass.

"Almost like a mirror," she murmured, bringing the half closer. And indeed, reflected back at her was the image of her own face, pale but slightly smudged from the morning's exertions.

But Micki had no time to gaze in wonder at this phenomenon, for already the image in the stone had begun to change. Once again there was the rippling of waves, and her reflection dissolved into a pattern of little lights. The image that replaced it was one that made Micki draw in her breath.

For it was no longer a reflection. It was an actual moving image, like a scene from a film. At first she could only make out the vague shapes of two people. Then she realized that one of them was herself. The other was her sister Jenny. They were sitting on the couch in the living room. Jenny was crying over something she was holding in her hand.

"I broke it, Micki," she sobbed.

Micki put her arm around her sister.

"Jenny, it's okay."

"But it's Mommy's birthday present. Now she'll think I don't love her. She'll think only you do." At that moment, their father entered the room, smiling and leading his wife by the hand.

"Present time!" he shouted gaily. Jenny looked heartbroken.

"Happy birthday, Mommy," said Micki. "This is from me and Jenny." She handed her a box wrapped in bright red and yellow paper. The change of expression on Jenny's face was perfect. It was as if the sun had come down and personally wiped away all her tears. Quietly she shoved her broken gift down the crack in the couch, and the image in the stone faded.

Micki smiled fondly. That had been two years ago. She still remembered the warm glowing feeling that she'd had through the whole day. Her mother had given her a big hug when she had tucked her into bed that night. Micki had never told her about what she'd done, but she wondered if her mother knew anyway.

Now another scene was coming into focus. It was on the playground of Micki's school. There were a lot of children yelling and running about, so it must have been morning recess. Micki noticed one group of children at the corner of the school yard who had formed a loose circle around something. Most of them were pupils from her own class, and she saw that she was one of the crowd. Louis Berry, the biggest and meanest boy in the class, was pointing scornfully to a chubby girl with glasses who stood in the middle of the circle.

"You're so fat, you jiggle like a bowl of jelly!" he shouted. The crowd laughed uproariously.

"Yeah, what does your mother feed you for breakfast, lard?" joined in another boy. The girl had begun to cry silently, huge tears running down her cheeks to her chin. She didn't even bother to brush them away.

"Crybaby, crybaby!" sang out Melanie Simon. Melanie was blond, pretty, and very popular, and the other children in the circle began to follow her example, chanting "Crybaby! Crybaby! Fatso is a crybaby!"

"Stop it, all of you!" Micki looked more closely at the picture to see who that brave person was who spoke. Then she saw herself step into the center of the circle and put her arm around the weeping girl. She stared out defiantly at the crowd.

"Bullies! Stop picking on Patricia! She's never done anything to you. Why don't you just leave her alone?" There were a lot of scornful retorts and jeering remarks directed at both Micki and the unfortunate Patricia, but they were forced and awkward. The crowd soon drifted away, grumbling with embarrassment, and as the scene faded, Micki could just glimpse the girl's grateful face, smiling through her tears.

Micki was puzzled. The mirror had just shown her a scene that had never happened. She didn't even know a Patricia. She wondered if this was something that was going to happen to her in the future. But she shook her head in disbelief. She didn't think she could ever be so brave as to stand up against all those people to defend a fat girl. They certainly were mean, though. It made her blood boil just watching them.

Micki had no idea how long she sat there looking at the pictures fade into and out of the mirror in the stone. Some of the things she saw had actually happened to her. Others were scenes she didn't recognize. But always she was doing something kind and admirable. In one of the pictures she wasn't even there, but in it were two of her mother's friends saying things like "Isn't Louise Silver's oldest a wonderful child?" Micki felt as if she could watch the mirror all day—it was better than the movies.

Finally the scenes stopped and the mirror rippled back to the rough surface of the stone egg. Reluctantly, she put it down.

"I wonder if the mirror in the other half has any nice pictures," she said, curiously picking it up. It felt slightly warm, as if it had been baking in the sun, though the place where it had been lying was well shaded. Yes, the mirror was still there, and it had started rippling. Micki propped the stone up against the tree and lay down on her stomach, her chin in her hands, as if she were getting ready to watch one of her favorite programs on television.

When the rippling motion had subsided, Micki once again saw herself pictured in the stone. This time the view was a close-up of her face. It was distinctly unpleasant. Her mouth was puckered into an angry pout, her jaw thrust forward defiantly. Then the focus shifted back and she could see that she was sitting huddled in the rocking chair in her bedroom at home.

"Micki, I want you to apologize to your mother." It was her father speaking. He was standing in the doorway, his hand on the doorknob.

"No." Her voice was mean and sullen.

"Micki, you know that was a terrible thing to say."

"I don't care. It's true. I do hate her." And she began rocking furiously back and forth in the chair. Her father shook his head sadly and left the room, closing the door behind him. But not before he turned and she could see the hurt look in his eyes.

Micki remembered the incident. It had been only a couple of months ago, when she had decided to run away from home. She'd filled her backpack with two pairs of jeans, some T-shirts, underwear, pajamas, her toothbrush, a box of granola bars, eight celery sticks with peanut butter wrapped in aluminum foil, Frederick, her stuffed donkey, and all the money from her piggy bank. She had actually got halfway to the bus before her mother came after her and hauled her kicking and screaming back to the house. Later she realized that she was glad her mother had found her and brought her back, but she refused to admit this to her parents. Instead she spent the evening closed up in her room, stuffing herself with celery sticks and granola bars. She felt quite sick after that, but when she tried to go to sleep and forget about it, she kept rolling over onto hard crumbs of rolled oats.

Micki didn't feel very comfortable about being reminded of that day. But she felt even worse when other scenes followed: In every one of them, there she was, scowling and sullen, angry and mean. As with the first mirror, sometimes the pictures were of things that had actually happened, sometimes not. But finally there came a scene that made Micki shrink with shame.

The picture was of the Silvers' basement. It had

been gaily decorated with streamers and party favors, and a big sign hung across the wall reading, "Happy Birthday Jenny." A dozen little girls in pointed birthday hats were laughing and scurrying about. In one corner of the room the children had built an elaborate playhouse out of cardboard boxes, folding chairs, blankets, a cleaning bucket, and a soup kettle. The house was open at the front, and inside one could see a large pink birthday cake resting on the unzipped sleeping bag that served as the rug, table, and chairs all in one.

Suddenly Micki saw herself descending the stairs at the back of the room. She stopped halfway down and, folding her arms across her chest, surveyed the scene of her sister's birthday party. She did not look happy about it.

"Micki! Come have some birthday cake in our new house," Jenny called gaily, her face flushed pink as her cake with the excitement of the day.

"No way!" scoffed Micki. She glared disdainfully at her sister's friends, as one by one they stopped what they were doing and glanced up at her anxiously.

"Hey!" yelled Micki. "That's *my* sleeping bag!"

"We didn't think you'd mind," explained Jenny. "Besides, you weren't playing with it."

"Well I am *now*!" Micki shot back. And with that she reached into the house, grabbed the sleeping bag, and gave a terrific tug. Jenny screamed as the fragile playhouse came tumbling down into a big heap atop her strawberry ice-cream cake. But Micki, taking no notice of her sister's distress, flounced upstairs in triumph, a dozen pairs of sorrowful eyes following her as she went. Then the scene faded into blankness.

"No!" Micki cried, her face wet with tears. "That's not me! I never did that! I'm not like that!" She glared at the offending stone, and before another picture could come into view, she picked it up and hurled it toward the water with all her strength. The stone traveled a surprising distance, almost to the center of the lake. It hissed angrily when it hit the water, and little bubbles of hot steam rose from the spot before the surface of the lake grew calm once more.

All of a sudden Micki realized that there was a terrible throbbing sensation in her hand. She looked down and saw a searing red welt across her palm. She reached for the other half of the stone egg, which lay at her feet. Immediately a coolness filled her body and her hand became less painful.

At that moment Micki was seized by an overwhelming desire to sleep. She wished she could sleep so deeply that no thoughts or visions would be able to reach her. In fact, she was secretly hoping that if only she could go to sleep right this instant, she might awaken to find this whole terrible morning had simply been a bad dream. For

Micki had already forgotten the good parts of the morning—how the first stone had shown her such pleasant images. All she could remember was the horrible hot stone and the frightful person it had revealed.

She threw herself down at the base of the pine tree, clutching the good half of the stone egg. She laid her cheek against it, feeling its cool roughness against her skin. As soon as Micki's face touched the stone, her surroundings seemed to grow fuzzy, almost as if a huge wad of cotton were being wrapped loosely around her. She opened her eyes, but all she could see was a glowing whiteness. She took a deep breath. The air was close and hot. She tried to sit up, but her arms and legs had become tangled in something that grew tighter when she struggled. It was a strangely familiar feeling, but she couldn't place it.

Then she realized what it was. She was caught inside a twisted web of sheets and blankets. It was something that happened to her often when she was having a bad dream at night. She was scrunched so far down toward the bottom of the bed that she could hardly breathe. She wrenched the sheets away from her and sat up with a start.

The morning sunlight was pouring in through the window. The window of her very own room.

8

Stories from the Past

Micki's first thought was that it had all been an incredible dream, and she felt an enormous sense of relief. But when she went over it again, it didn't seem possible. Everything was too vivid and real—the house, the attic bedroom, Sarah, and especially the old woman. Micki shuddered at the memory of that cackling laugh, and covered her face with her hands. They had a funny, earthy smell, and she looked at them curiously. Why, they were filthy! Little bits of mud were caked under her fingernails. She pulled aside the blankets. The bed was sprinkled with pine needles.

Micki jumped into the sweatpants and T-shirt that were lying across her chair and raced to the bathroom. For five whole minutes she furiously scrubbed her hands and face until they were spotlessly clean. When she examined her hands for telltale signs of dirt, she noticed that her right palm was covered with a dull red patch, like an old scar.

The sound of movement below told Micki that someone was already awake. For a moment she wondered why no one had come running when they had heard her up and about. Then she rushed breathlessly downstairs, trying to imagine how on earth she would be able to explain to her parents where she had been. She found her father alone in the kitchen. He was washing up the breakfast dishes and looked around at her smiling, his yellow rubber gloves encased in soapy bubbles.

"Hello, sweetheart," he said affectionately. "Feeling better this morning? You've been asleep for hours." Micki glanced at the kitchen clock above the refrigerator. It was nearly ten o'clock. But ten o'clock on what day? Her father seemed perfectly normal. He didn't act as if she'd been gone for two weeks at all.

"Where is everyone?" she asked in an offhand manner.

"Long gone. Your mother and Jenny are off shopping for the trip. They won't be be back 'til late this afternoon."

"What trip?" Micki looked at her father blankly.

"Good heavens, Micki, where have you been! We're going to the cottage on the lake tomorrow, remember?"

Of course. The lake. It had completely slipped her mind. She and Jenny had been looking forward to this trip ever since their father had read an article about lakeside holidays and proposed the idea as a way to spend their spring vacation.

Micki did a quick calculation. Her parents had arranged to leave on Monday to avoid the holiday traffic. That meant that today was only Sunday, and yesterday must have been the Saturday of their visit to the toy museum. No wonder her father didn't act worried or surprised to see her. Just one night had gone by after all!

"You must be pretty hungry, or you couldn't have forgotten about going to the lake. It's all I've been hearing about for weeks," her father grinned. Micki looked at him with puzzlement. Last night's dinner at the DeSilvers' had been unusually late, so she really wasn't the least bit hungry. Then she remembered guiltily that as far as her father was concerned, she'd been sent upstairs the previous evening without any supper. It all seemed ages ago.

"That depends on what's for breakfast," she replied somewhat defensively, yanking open the refrigerator door with only mild interest. It was disappointingly bare.

"There's toast and strawberry jam or cereal."

"Porridge and cream?" she asked, brightening at the mention of cereal. Her father looked at her sharply.

"What do you think this is, a restaurant?" he said. "Cereal means *cold* cereal. There's a box in the cupboard."

"Yuck," said Micki, wrinkling her nose in distaste. After the magnificent breakfasts at the DeSilvers', toast and jam or dry cereal seemed a poor choice indeed. "I guess I'll have cereal," she added quickly when she saw her father's stern expression.

She fetched a bowl and spoon and sat down at the kitchen table. Stirring listlessly, she watched the milk seep into the bran flakes, turning them soft and soggy the way she liked them. Her father had gone back to the dishes and was humming quietly to himself.

Micki's thoughts wandered to her experiences of the last two weeks. She was positive that she hadn't imagined those two weeks, yet everything seemed to have vanished so completely. All that was left was a vague sense of foreboding, like a shadow or a cloud at the back of her mind. She felt as if the cloud were hiding something—something that it was crucial for her to remember.

"Well, Micki, what would you like to do this morning?" said her father as he gave the counter a final wipe with the sponge. "We have the rest of the day to ourselves—it's just us chickens."

Chickens! Micki gave an involuntary shudder. Suddenly she heard the voice of the old woman as if it had emerged from behind the cloud in her mind. "Ask your father, chicken, ask your father." She rubbed her palms nervously on her sweatpants and felt something hard in her pocket.

That's funny, she thought, I don't remember putting anything in there. And it's so heavy. How could I not have noticed it before? She drew the object out and stared. It was one half of the old woman's stone egg. Micki placed it on the kitchen table as a jumble of images came rushing into her head. She hoped fervently that it was the good half of the egg that lay before her, but the smooth round surface glistening in the morning sunlight gave her no clue.

"Daddy," she said slowly, as if in a trance, "which comes first, the chicken or the egg?" She looked up at her father. He was staring mutely at the stone egg, his face pale and expressionless.

"Where did you get that?" he whispered hoarsely.

"An old woman gave it to me," she replied,

watching him. "Then she said, 'Go to the source. Branch to the trunk. Ask your father.' Daddy, do you have any idea what she meant?"

Micki's father looked hard at her but said nothing. Then he stood up, walked distractedly across the room, and stared out the window for a long time. His glance appeared to be directed up at the branches of the large maple tree in the neighbors' front lawn. Its pale-green leaves had just begun to unfurl.

"Can this really be happening?" he muttered to himself, running a hand through his dark hair in a way that made the widow's peak stand out on his forehead. He appeared to be engaged in some kind of inner argument.

"Micki, I must confess that just thinking how you come to ask me such a question makes me feel ill at ease. But something also tells me that refusing to answer you would be foolish. So let me tell you a story—a true story—about a little boy." He seated himself at the kitchen table and adjusted his chair to face his daughter. Then he leaned forward and began speaking with an earnest expression.

"It was many years ago, and the boy was seven years old at the time. His father had been sent overseas, and while he was away, the boy's mother died very suddenly. The boy had no relatives except for a great-grandfather who lived in a big old house in the country. So he was sent to live in the big old house until his father could return and take care of him."

"Daddy," said Micki intently, "that little boy was you, wasn't it? It's okay, you don't have to pretend."

Mr. Silver's eyes narrowed as he looked at his daughter, but then his gaze softened. "Very well, Michelle," he said gently. "That little boy was me.

"It was a very lonely summer. I was given an enormous attic room with two little old wooden beds that looked like they came with the house. I remember wishing there was another boy to sleep in the other bed so I could have somebody to talk to when I was sent up to that dark, empty room every night.

"During the day I preferred to escape the old mansion. I spent a lot of time wandering about the beautiful woods behind the house. Sometimes I'd spend the whole day swimming in the little lake on the property, where I'd also hunt for tadpoles. There wasn't a soul to talk to except the cook and a few elderly servants. My great-grandfather was ailing and kept mostly to his room.

"The house was very remote, and no one ever came to visit. In my memory the whole summer is like one long blur of isolation. But there are two incidents that I remember very clearly. Or, to be more precise, there are two incidents that I'd forgotten I remembered, if you know what I mean. Until just yesterday. Perhaps you know why better than I."

Here Micki's father paused and looked at her questioningly, but she remained motionless, her eyes glued to his face. He sighed and continued.

"As I was saying, it was rare for anyone to set foot in that old house. Maybe that's why the visits from the Egg Lady stand out in my mind. She was the oldest woman I think I'd ever seen. Her skin was a deep brown, like well-tanned leather. And she had the darkest, most penetrating eyes. They seemed to just look right through me. The first time she came to the door with her basket of eggs, I'm sure I must have fled in terror.

"But I think my very boredom with those long, lazy summer days must have given me courage. Because by the time a month had gone by, I'd begun to look forward to the appearance of the Egg Lady with a kind of fascination. And I must say that 'appearance' is the proper word, because the Egg Lady seemed to materialize out of thin air—no one ever saw her coming, and she had no set schedule. But somehow, just when the household was running out of eggs, she'd show up as if she'd been summoned.

"The eggs she used to bring!" Mr. Silver exclaimed, his eyes shimmering at the distant memory. "Nothing like the boring, tasteless things we buy in the supermarket today—fit only for making pancakes. In fact, nothing like I could remember ever getting in my house in the city. She always had freshly laid chicken eggs, of course, but also duck eggs with bright yellow yokes, and goose eggs, tiny speckled quail eggs, even pheasant eggs. But there was no ordering in advance or anything like that. We took whatever she brought. 'Each according to his deserts,' I can remember she used to say, as if the eggs she brought us were some kind of divine judgment.

"The occasion that I recall with such particular vividness was a very stormy day toward the end of August, shortly before my return to school and life in the city. There was no thought of going outside on one of my solitary jaunts—the skies had simply opened up, and thunder and lightning encased the house with a fury. At a loss for anything better to do, I was down in the kitchen helping the cook with her preparations for the midday meal— though probably being more of a hindrance than anything else—when there came an insistent knocking at the door of the servants' entrance.

"'Who in heaven's name could that be on an evil day like this!' exclaimed the cook, bustling across

111

the kitchen to find out. 'Why goodness me, it's you! And to think that I'd just begun rearranging my menu because I'd not got enough eggs for the old man's custard this evening!' And flinging the door open, she gratefully ushered in the Egg Lady.

"That anyone in her right mind would choose such a day to go delivering eggs—let alone such a frail old woman—only served to increase my fascination with the Egg Lady. But all the same I kept my distance and stayed safely as an observer on my side of the kitchen.

"The old woman followed the cook into the kitchen and laid her basket on the table, removing the linen cloth that protected her precious burden. We must have been the first people she called on that day, because it was heavy and brimming with eggs of all different sizes and colors. The cook, hands on her hips, stared greedily at the plentiful selection. Then, noticing the sorry state of the Egg Lady's dripping cloak, she hastened to remove the garment and carry it into the back room behind the boiler, where it could dry more quickly.

"It seemed as though the Egg Lady had been waiting for this moment all along. While she had appeared not to notice me when she entered the room, she turned immediately toward me now and beckoned me with a gnarled forefinger. I cowered in the corner, not once letting my eyes leave her face.

"'Ah, now he's afraid, he that's been watching me these many weeks,' she crooned. 'Come closer, boy. It's not I that would harm you.' I remember feeling the magnetism of her eyes and had no choice but to obey.

"'Closer, closer,' she urged, until I had crept so close that I could see the little red lines that traveled across the whites of her eyes, like arrows pointing to the back of her head. She raised one knotted brown hand and laid it on my shoulder. Her grip was surprisingly strong for such an old woman, but as soon as she touched me, I felt a cold shudder pass through my entire body. Those eyes were boring into me as if they were looking for something that even I didn't know I was hiding.

"'So this is what the line has come to,' she said at last. 'Little Bobby Silver, are you worth your mettle? No matter, no matter. It's the girls— daughters, my boy—they can end the family. Keep an eye on yours.' Then she reached way into the bottom of her basket and drew out something round and heavy and pressed it into my hand. It was a stone egg. It looked exactly like that one there," Micki's father added in an awed tone.

"When she gave me the stone, she looked at me with a very faint smile and said: 'The chicken or the egg—do you think you know which comes first? You don't.'

"No sooner had the old woman spoken those

mysterious words than the cook returned and she lapsed into silence. She went away without even waiting until her cloak was dry, leaving me her odd gift."

"Daddy," Micki said thoughtfully when her father had finished, "whatever happened to that stone egg?"

"I kept it," he replied. "At night I used to sleep with it under my pillow, and during the day I would take it out and just stare at it. If I left my room, the egg was sure to be in my pocket. I even brought it with me when I went to play at the lake, so reluctant was I to let it out of my sight. In fact, it was at the lake that I saw the last of my beautiful egg." He sighed.

"What happened?"

"Well, one day, right before I was to return to the city, I went to the lake for the last time. But no sooner had I rolled up my trouser legs and sunk my bare toes into the oozy mud when I realized I wasn't alone. I turned just in time to see the Egg Lady removing the stone egg from inside my shoe, where I had left it.

"'You won't be needing this anymore, chicken,' she said, popping it neatly into her basket. 'As long as you remember what you've been told.' And with that she seemed to virtually disappear into the tree. I never saw her again after that."

"Never?" breathed Micki.

Her father hesitated. "No . . . At least I don't think so. Unless—but no, it couldn't be . . ."

"Unless what?" persisted Micki.

"Well, the strangest thing is," said her father, giving way to the urgent tone in his daughter's voice, "I feel as if I saw someone very like her just recently. And yet my reason tells me it's not possible. Why, the Egg Lady must have been well into her eighties even then."

"When did you think you saw her?"

"Why, just yesterday at the toy museum. That old woman who let us in. It's funny—they didn't exactly *look* the same, and yet there was something that made me think them very much alike."

Micki's head spun. Everything seemed somehow connected, but it still made no sense. There were so many unanswered questions.

"Daddy, why do you think the Egg Lady took your egg back?"

"I used to ponder that one quite a bit. In a way, I think it was good that she did. In just a few weeks, I'd become strangely obsessed with that piece of stone. But the only thing I can think of is that the egg had served its purpose—which brings me to my other great memory of that summer."

"Yes?" prompted Micki eagerly.

Micki's father took a deep breath. Once more he

115

looked closely at his daughter, and then continued with his story.

"The second incident concerns my great-grandfather. As I mentioned, he was a very old man at the time. He was quite frail and nearly bedridden, so I'd only seen him once or twice, when he was well enough to come downstairs. But one day, shortly after my encounter with the Egg Lady, I received a summons to come see him in his private quarters.

"I'd never been to that part of the house. His bedroom was situated way at the back on the second floor but could be easily reached by a little-used staircase leading up from the study below. I followed the nurse upstairs, fingering the stone egg in my pocket for comfort as had become my habit. She seemed reluctant to be bringing me into the sickroom, but apparently her objections had been overruled.

"'The old gentleman simply won't lie still,' she grumbled. 'He's been calling out to see "the lad who's been brought here" until he's made himself sick, so I'm finally giving in and allowing you to visit him against my better judgment. But mind you say nothing to upset the poor dear or you'll be out on your ear before you know what's hit you,' she added sternly.

"Well she needn't have been concerned on that

account. My great-grandfather was ancient enough to inspire my terror, and I had no intention of uttering a solitary word. When we'd reached the old man's bedroom, I felt positively weak, and at that point I'm not sure that I could have spoken even if addressed directly.

"The room, when we entered, was oppressively dark. The shutters were closed tightly, and the only light came from an old lamp with a tattered shade at the opposite end of the room. There was a heavy medicinal smell in the air. The nurse led me to the huge four-poster bed where my great-grandfather lay, looking very frail among all the pillows and bedclothes. I stood for some time looking down at him, but he seemed fast asleep, and I didn't dare awaken him.

"But it was not a peaceful sleep. I hadn't been there more than two minutes before he began tossing and turning and muttering inaudibly. He seemed possessed by some kind of horrible dream, because I kept hearing him repeat, over and over again, the phrase 'Look out for the tree!'

"Then suddenly he was startled into wakefulness. He sat straight up in his bed, opened his eyes wide, and stared directly into my face. At first he appeared confused and didn't recognize me. But once he'd regained his composure, I had little doubt that he knew exactly who I was.

"'Hello, boy,' he said, his eyes beginning to focus steadily on my face.

"'Hello, sir,' I mumbled. It was all I could manage.

"He said nothing for some time. But from the way he kept grasping repeatedly at the bedclothes, I could tell he had something on his mind. His eyes kept clouding and unclouding, and he seemed to be making a strenuous effort to collect his thoughts. Finally he started to talk in a rambling manner, and I was never quite sure which of his comments were directed toward me and which toward the world at large.

"'There's many a tree that may seem strong, but it's the roots below the ground that can rot before you know it. It's the roots, yes, the roots that make the man. But a broken branch can kill the roots,' he said, clutching at his leg and wincing in pain. 'Keep your eye on the branch.'

"For a moment he lay panting, as though the effort had been too much for him. I was extremely nervous and frightened, and to calm my nerves I had brought out my stone egg. I rubbed it first with one hand, then with the other. Perhaps I was hoping it could magically enable me to disappear from the crazy old man's bedside. It was some moments before I realized that my great-grandfather was now completely alert and staring straight at the egg.

"'Whole again,' he whispered. And for the first time he smiled. But immediately he seemed to remember something, and quick as lightning he reached out his hand, caught hold of my shirt front, and pulled me right up close to his face with surprising strength.

"'Warn your girl it must be made whole again,' he rasped, gesturing to the egg, which I now clutched to my chest for dear life. 'It must be made whole again, or it will be the end of the line.' Then he released me and collapsed against the pillows mumbling incoherently.

"The old man was obviously delirious, and the nurse blamed me for what appeared to be a worsening of his condition. She led me away with a great deal of loud complaining about the impossible nature of little boys.

"I never saw my great-grandfather again. Soon afterward I returned to the city. I later learned that following my visit he had sunk into a coma and died within a matter of days. Eventually the old house was sold, and my father told me it was later demolished to make way for a resort community.

"After that I completely forgot about my great-grandfather. From time to time I've remembered our conversation, but never with anything approaching understanding. In fact, I still have no idea what he was getting at, but maybe it wasn't such a bunch of nonsense after all. Perhaps he really was trying to tell me something. And I can't help thinking he was meant to see that stone egg."

Micki had not moved from her seat, and her knuckles were white from gripping the edge of the kitchen table.

"Daddy," she said grimly, "who was your great-grandfather?"

"His name was Gregory DeSilver. His son, my grandfather, had the 'De' dropped from our surname before he married my grandmother."

Gregory. So Gregory was her great-great-grandfather. But just the other evening, when Dr. Bain had paid his nightly visit, he had expressed the sober opinion that unless there was a miracle, Gregory would most certainly die.

At that moment Micki knew she had to get back to the DeSilvers. With a cold horror she realized that if Gregory were to die, she herself would never be born.

9

The Lake

Micki lay in bed trying to sort out everything her father had told her. Thoughts whizzed about like little freight cars speeding off in all different directions. She was abominably confused. Surely, since she was here, that was proof that her great-great-grandfather Gregory must have survived his illness and lived to have children. So she needn't worry. But perhaps the only way he did survive was through the intercession of his cousin Michelle. As far as Micki knew, that person was herself. Therefore she must have actually done something to save Gregory's life some ninety years before she was even born! By the same token, she thought guiltily, she must have done something to threaten his life many years after he died a very old man! The contradictions made her head spin.

"But what if now I do nothing?" she thought. "Surely I can't be 'unborn'?" Then something horrible occurred to her. She seemed to hear, almost as if she were making the remark now, her own voice speak the words "I *wish* I'd never been born!" Had she said such a thing? She knew that she had.

"But I was just *kidding*!" she cried aloud. No, she forced the idea from her mind. It was impossible. She was *real*. Her father and mother were *real*. Jenny was *real*. Everything up to the present had already happened, so what could she possibly do to change it? Yes, perhaps after all it was best to do nothing. Just wait.

All these thoughts swirled about in her mind, and they seemed to collect and gather momentum like a growing storm. As she drifted off to sleep at last, Micki felt as if she had been sucked into the vortex of the storm, so that it was not merely ideas but she herself who was spinning relentlessly around.

"Or maybe I am an idea," she found herself thinking.

"Precisely, chicken," said a familiar voice. Turning, Micki shrank to see the old woman holding a staff before her and gesturing toward a beach, where the storm was becoming more insistent. Mutely, Micki followed her. The wind was churning the sand so fiercely that it stung Micki's cheeks and caused her eyes to water. The noise it made as it ripped through the dunes and beat back against the angry waves was like an endless, high-pitched scream. Yet when the old woman spoke, Micki could hear every word perfectly.

"So you think the past cannot be altered?" she said in a faint mocking tone. "A life," she rasped, casting her staff in the sand and scooping out a small impression, "what if all of a sudden...it wasn't?" Instantly the hole disappeared, replaced by the sand that had surrounded it. The wind recast the surface with more sand, and no trace of the hole remained.

"Such would be the way!" she almost gloated. Suddenly the wind subsided and the waves withdrew silently into the ocean. "Can you afford to take such a chance, Micki Silver?" she whispered hoarsely, and before Micki could reply, the woman had disappeared into the black night. Micki tried to call out, but her voice froze in her throat.

She woke up to find her face pressed deep into

the pillow, her arms folded above her head as if shielding her from some unseen terror. The gray dawn light filtered weakly through the sheer curtains. Micki had half expected to wake up in Sarah's attic bedroom, but the familiar shapes of her own bureau and rocking chair told her otherwise. It was still too early to rise, so she tossed fitfully for some time. Finally, when she could stand it no longer, she got up, threw on some clothes, and tiptoed downstairs.

She was surprised to find her father already up and starting to pack the car for their trip.

"Couldn't sleep?" he asked with a wan smile. He looked tired.

"No."

"Me either. So I figured what's the point of lying about in bed? Might as well get up and get packing. Like to give me a hand?"

Micki nodded. For a while they carried out suitcases and parcels in silence and stacked them in the garage next to the station wagon. Then her father opened a cabinet in the pantry and began to take down a cardboard chest labeled "Car Games." This assortment of boxes, cards, and booklets was reserved especially for long car trips. The family never touched it on any other occasion. And each time they set off on one of these trips, their father was sure to have scoured the shops in search of a car game they'd never played.

There was a strict rule that the new game was never played first. It was important to wait until the old games had begun to pall, and everyone was becoming irritable from the long ride. Then their mother would reach into the chest and say, "I wonder what your father has up his sleeve this time." For a while Micki and Jenny would be engrossed in the new game and forget to quarrel and misbehave.

"This box is getting so full, I think we're going to have to start prioritizing," said Mr. Silver. He brought it down with a thud. It was brimming with bits and pieces of games accumulated over the years.

"Here, Micki, help me sort this stuff out. We can't possibly need all of it." He turned the chest upside down, emptying its contents into a pile on the floor. Micki reached for a small plastic bag on top and drew out an unopened box.

"Ooh, Daddy, is this the new game?" she asked excitedly.

"Now Micki, you know that's supposed to be a surprise," replied her father, quickly taking the box from her. Then he stopped and stared.

"That's strange," he said. "This isn't what I bought at all. They must have given me the wrong thing at the store." He handed it to Micki, forgetting it was supposed to be a surprise. On the outside, in large green letters, was the title of the game, Trace Your Family Tree. Underneath was a picture of a large tree with roots spreading out beneath the soil, and branches reaching up to a painted sky. Each part of the tree was labeled with the name of a different generation, starting with the oldest generation at the roots.

"Not much of a car game," he muttered in annoyance. But Micki could see from his face that the mistaken purchase had rattled his nerves.

"Micki," he said, laying a hand on her arm, "I have no idea how that thing got into my bag. It seems an unfortunate coincidence in light of our conversation yesterday."

"What do you mean?"

"Well, I've been thinking quite a bit about what I told you. In fact, I've been thinking about it half the night. You see, I don't want you to get the wrong idea—all this business about daughters destroying the family name and preserving the family tree." He shoved the box angrily back in the bag.

"In my humble opinion," he continued, "it's absolute bunk. I've never given a hoot for that kind of thing. As far as I'm concerned, if I'm the last Silver on earth, that's fine with me. I'm proud to have two wonderful daughters."

Micki stared at him, uncomprehending. Then it occurred to her that her father had completely missed the point of what his great-grandfather and the Egg Lady were telling him all those years ago. Why, he seemed to think the whole thing had to do with having daughters instead of sons who would pass the family name on to their children. Or was that just what he wanted to believe because it was a simpler, less frightening explantion? But Micki knew there was more to it than that.

"Now I'm going to take this silly game back to the shop this instant," he said briskly, overlooking the fact that it was still only seven o'clock in the morning.

"Oh no, Daddy! May I please keep it?" Micki asked. She had a strong conviction that the game was meant for her.

Her father looked at her dubiously. "All right, Micki, but I really know very little about our family history, so don't expect me to be of much help to you," he replied unhappily.

"That's okay," Micki murmured, barely conscious of his response. As soon as her father left the room to carry more things out to the garage, she ripped open the cellophane wrapping and pulled out the contents of the box. Inside there was an instruction card with a picture of a tree identical to the one on the outside. The card had been partially filled in with names so that it could serve as a guide for the user.

But when Micki peered more closely at the names, she gasped in disbelief. This wasn't an example card at all—the names were those of her own family! Among the roots of the tree the name Gregory DeSilver had been inserted in bold black handwriting. At the top of the trunk, where the tree divided into branches, was her father's name. And along two of the smaller branches on the right-hand side were the names Michelle and Jennifer Silver.

Suddenly Micki remembered something. She could hear the words almost as if they were being repeated to her now—the old woman's cryptic rhyme:

> *The branch once turned to the trunk and said,*
> *'Though it's not my wish to see you dead,*
> *I'd so much rather we severed ties.'*
> *But in snapping free the whole tree dies.*

What if the tree, just as Sarah had said, was not a *real* tree? Or even a particular person. What if it meant the *family* tree? And *she* was the branch? She had certainly wanted to be free of her family quite recently. But how would that make the whole tree die? Anyway, Micki argued with herself, she hadn't actually "snapped free," because here she was, back home again and getting ready to go on a trip with her family.

Then another fragment of the old woman's conversation came back to her: "Sometimes a wish can kill." What if that were true? What if, simply by wishing, she had set into motion a course of events over which she had no control? Micki felt a sudden chill deep inside, and she shivered in the early-morning sunshine.

During the first part of the trip, everyone was fairly quiet. When they left the house it was quite early, and Jenny had fallen back to sleep, her small fists closed tightly, supporting her cheek against the side of the car. Micki turned and watched her sister for a few moments. It seemed hard to believe that she had ever been so angry with her.

"I'll make it up to her," she said to herself. "I'll take her wading in the lake, and I'll give her my tadpoles if I find any." She continued to imagine more and more elaborate instances in which she would play the role of a model big sister, until even she wouldn't have recognized herself if they had ever come to pass.

Yet a nagging feeling remained. She tried not to think about it, but at the back of her mind Micki knew that the episode with the DeSilvers was not over. It wasn't that she didn't want to see her adopted family again. In fact, she quite missed Sarah. But she knew that when and if she found herself back with them, something would be expected of her. Something to do with Gregory. Something that she would find very difficult to achieve.

Micki reached into her book bag, where she had stashed the box with the family tree game. She drew out the card and gazed at it, hoping to find some clue to guide her. She swallowed hard. At the bottom of the tree, where the name of Gregory DeSilver had stood out boldly among its roots, the writing had now faded to a watery gray. And the roots themselves were less sturdy, as if they had begun to lose their grip in the soil.

As the day wore on, the trip went less smoothly. In spite of her earlier resolutions, Micki could not help embroiling herself in several loud quarrels with Jenny. In all fairness to Micki, Jenny was not on her best behavior and was responsible for initiating a number of the squabbles. When Jenny dropped crayon shavings down the back of Micki's T-shirt while she was quietly minding her own business and looking out the window, Micki was forced to give her a sharp smack in retaliation. To Micki the wailing that resulted was completely uncalled for. Nevertheless, it landed her in hot water with her parents. Jenny was taken, weeping inconsolably, to sit in her mother's lap, and Micki was left alone in the backseat to sulk.

For the first time since her return, she felt that familiar black mood descend on her. She began to brood on the unfairness of her treatment and to wish she could go somewhere else where people appreciated her. Micki looked up and caught sight of her father's face in the rearview mirror. When their eyes met, he winked at her and flashed her one of his irresistible smiles. At that moment he reminded her of Sarah, and it was impossible to stay angry.

"What about a game?" her father suggested, and Micki's mother pulled out the game box from where it was resting under her feet. Before long the entire family was engrossed in the familiar car games, and peace reigned until everyone but Micki's mother, who had taken over the driving, had nodded off to sleep. No one even seemed to notice that there was no new game this time, and certainly neither Micki nor her father felt obliged to mention it. After all, it was their secret.

The family reached their destination late that evening. The full moon made the sky so bright that they had little difficulty finding the cottage in spite of its seclusion.

Everyone was too tired to do much more than look the house over briefly and drag in the few things they would need during the night. Micki tumbled into bed without even bothering to unpack her pajamas. Cuddled under the soft down-filled comforter, she was soon fast asleep.

When she woke up the next day, Micki jumped out of bed and ran to the bedroom window. She could just glimpse the lake in the distance below. Little glints of the morning sunlight reflected off the water through the trees. She looked around the room. It was cheerful, but small. Everything— the walls, the ceiling, even the floors—was built from broad planks of knotted pine, and the whole room gave off the scent of freshly cut timber.

Jenny was still asleep in the bed across from her. Micki was not sure she was going to like sharing a room with her sister, but it was part of the bargain both girls had made with their parents.

Micki ambled downstairs to the living room. Both her parents were already up and unloading the car. Micki went outside to give them a hand. The morning air was clear and cool. It would probably be too cold to go swimming in the lake, but they could certainly go wading, and their father could take them out in the boat that came with the cottage. Micki and Jenny had been planning these fishing excursions for weeks.

"Can we go to the lake now?" Micki asked eagerly.

"Why don't we wait until after breakfast, sweetheart?" replied her father. Micki knit her brows in disappointment. She didn't want to wait until after breakfast. She wanted her holiday to begin *now*.

"It's all right, Robert," said her mother. "Why don't the two of you go ahead down. I'll stay here with Jenny and get started on breakfast. I'm sure the lake is lovely at this hour of the morning."

"Okay, Micki, let's go!" said her father, swinging his arm merrily over her shoulder.

Micki threw her mother a grateful smile, and they set off. The path to the lake was well worn but quite narrow. It wound downward through the forest of fragrant evergreens until the trees gave way to a small clearing matted with soft pine needles. Beyond the clearing, a perfect little blue-green lake rippled gently in the sunlight.

Micki and her father stood gazing at the lake for a long while, hardly daring to breathe. Then they looked at each other, though neither of them spoke. But each was thinking the same thing. Each was thinking that they had been in this place before.

There was no mistaking it. It was the lake at the bottom of the DeSilver property.

10

In the Woods

Micki and her father were extremely silent throughout breakfast, and her mother looked at them curiously more than once. Jenny, oblivious as usual, did most of the talking. She was determined that they should go fishing in the lake as early as possible, and everyone agreed that this was a good plan. So as soon as breakfast was over, Mr. Silver took Jenny in the car to the local tackle shop where they could rent fishing rods and buy bait.

Micki helped wash the dishes and bring in the

rest of the bags. Her mother was amazed at Micki's helpful manner but made no comment. Instead she suggested that they do up a really nice picnic lunch for later in the afternoon, with the food she had brought from home in the ice chest. Even though the lake was only a fifty-yard walk from the house, she said, bringing a picnic made it feel more like a real outing. Besides, she added, smiling, the last time they'd planned a picnic, things hadn't turned out all that well. Perhaps they could make up for it now. Micki looked a bit shamefaced and became very intent on drying the dishes.

When everything was clean in the kitchen, Micki went up to her room. She dutifully made her own bed and then glanced over at the tousled sheets of her sister's. Her first reaction was to be angry with Jenny for being such a slob. But she stopped herself.

"Good grief, she's only six!" she admonished. She couldn't remember making her own bed when she was six. In fact, she had to admit, she often didn't make her bed now, if only to annoy her mother.

Micki sighed and began straightening Jenny's bed as best she could. As long as there had to be two of them in the same room, she reasoned, she might as well make an effort to keep things neat.

The sun was now well above the trees, and a

long ray of golden light stretched at an angle across the floor, then up the side and top of Micki's bed. Micki lay on the bed, directly in the sunbeam's path, stretching her neck into its warmth. She reached under her pillow and pulled out the game card, which she had placed there the night before. She was hardly surprised to see that the letters of Gregory DeSilver's name had faded even more during the night. But what she found more disturbing was the rest of the picture. All the other names, including her own and Jenny's, had begun to fade as well.

"But what can I do?" she cried aloud.

Suddenly her thoughts turned to the lake. There was no doubt in her mind that this was the very same lake that had once been a part of the DeSilver property. She knew that her father, too, had recognized it from his boyhood. After all, hadn't he told her that following his great-grandfather's death, the estate had been sold and the land turned into a resort community? And another thing seemed certain: Her being here was no coincidence. The question was, why? She knew the only way to find out would be to go there herself. Alone.

Having made her decision, Micki set off for the lake with a pile of blankets and other supplies. Her mother said she would follow with the picnic basket as soon as her father and Jenny got back. Mrs. Silver wasn't very keen on the idea of fishing, but she'd brought a good book and her embroidery and was happy to watch the progress of her husband and daughters from the safety of dry land.

Micki veered left off the main path that she and her father had taken earlier and turned onto the little weather-beaten dock where the rowboat was moored. She had promised her mother she would not go near the boat until the others arrived. In fact, Micki was rather afraid of boats and not a very good swimmer, so she had no intention of getting into this rickety-looking specimen with no one else around. Instead she dumped everything on the dock and retraced her steps to the path that led to the clearing.

The air had warmed slightly, and Micki removed her shoes and socks to test the water. It was icy. She burrowed her feet deep into the brown mud and squished them about, trying to find some warmth.

"Ouch!" she cried aloud. Her foot had struck something hard. Carefully she prodded the object with her big toe. It gave way slightly and then was sucked back into the mud. Curious now, Micki reached down and felt around the object with her fingers. It was smooth and round. She dug beneath it in the mud. Its undersurface was flat and rough.

It was small, no bigger than her palm, but it was firmly lodged in the ooze. With both hands she created an air pocket so that the mud loosened its grip, and she was able to yank the object free. She examined it eagerly.

"Why, it's just an old rock!" she muttered in disappointment at having taken so much trouble to rescue it from the muck. She threw the rock down in disgust and watched as ripples of water lapped about it, washing the mud in little swirls from its surface.

There was something about the process that held Micki's attention. She couldn't tear herself away, much as she wanted to get onto dry land so she could warm her feet, which were going all numb. It was as if the mud spiralling off the stone were a smokescreen hiding something she needed to know. It wasn't until the speckled rose-colored rock was completely washed clean that Micki reached down, her hand trembling in recognition, to pick up half a stone egg.

She knew, even before she pulled out her own half from the nylon waist pack under her windbreaker, that the fit would be perfect. It was the horrible half of the egg that she had hurled into the middle of this very lake just two days ago. Two days ago, but also a hundred years ago, she reminded herself. And it had taken a hundred years for the rock to make its way back to the lake's edge, where it was waiting patiently for her to reclaim it.

Micki seated herself against the large pine tree at the edge of the lake. She held both halves of the egg in front of her and gazed at them, deep in thought. How had the bad half got back to her, like a boomerang coming full circle? More important, why? She was obviously meant to keep it, as well as the good half of the egg.

Reluctantly Micki thought back to the ugly pictures she had seen mirrored in the bad egg. In her anger she had refused to believe that the person she saw there was herself, but she knew in her heart that it was. Maybe not all the scenes were real, but the *feelings* were—she had had those feelings, and they had made her do mean, nasty things. But she had also had the feelings in the scenes from the good egg. Those were her, too.

"Both are a part of me," she murmured to herself, holding the two halves close together so that the crack became invisible. What was it that old Gregory DeSilver had told her father on his deathbed? "Warn your girl it must be made whole again, or it will be the end of the line." But how could it be made whole again, she wondered, now that it was so undeniably split into two halves?

As she continued musing, sitting with her back

to the tree, Micki began to have the most peculiar sensation. It was as if there was a gradual shift in her surroundings, and yet she could pinpoint no actual change. Then she realized what it was: She felt as though everything had grown somehow smaller—the tree she was leaning against seemed less sturdy, the forest floor less rich and tangled with undergrowth. A rustling noise sounded from behind her.

"Michelle, where *have* you been all morning?" It was Sarah. On one arm she carried a wicker basket over which was draped a brightly colored cloth.

Micki stared in disbelief. Her left hand had begun to throb dully. When she examined it, she saw that the red welt from the burn she had received two days ago looked fresh and angry. She also noticed that even though she hadn't felt the change, she was no longer wearing her jeans and windbreaker but her starched pinafore. She craned her neck forward. There was no sign of the dock or the rowboat.

"Mother has had Cook prepare us a lovely picnic," Sarah chattered on without waiting for an answer. "She's given us the day off from lessons, and you'll never guess why! Miss Collins has given notice—just like that! If you ask me, it's the best news we've had in weeks. I never could bear the miserable creature—but I think it was really the two of us together that finally sent her packing." Sarah giggled and gave Micki a delighted grin of complicity.

"Michelle, what is it?" Sarah's tone had changed to one of concern. "You look as if you've seen a ghost."

"How long have I been gone?" asked Micki, her voice trembling slightly.

"That depends on when you left," replied her cousin. "I didn't even hear you get up this morning. I kept thinking you'd be back soon, but I finally decided to go out and look for you. I didn't want to miss any more of the first beautiful morning we've had in days. It's already eleven o'clock."

So on this occasion, the amount of time passing was reversed—almost no time had gone by in the nineteenth century while Micki was living through two whole days in the twentieth. It was almost as if the time she had just left was waiting for her to return before it continued. Thus while everyone else went through one day, she went through two. At this rate, Micki thought dryly, she might be old enough to be thirteen by the time she was twelve!

Sarah had laid a tablecloth out on the ground and was already eagerly unpacking the picnic basket.

"I'm starving, aren't you?"

"No, I just ate," replied Micki without thinking.

141

"You did? When?" asked Sarah in a puzzled voice.

"Oh! I mean I ate a lot last night," Micki said quickly, trying to cover for her carelessness. But Sarah had stopped what she was doing and was leaning back on her heels, her arms folded firmly across her chest.

"Michelle DeSilver, whatever is wrong with you this morning?" She looked closely at Micki and then said, "I know what it is—you've seen *her*, haven't you?"

For a moment Micki looked puzzled. She had nearly forgotten about the old woman, so much had happened since their encounter.

"How did you know?"

"Because I saw her too—I mean, not actually, but last night when I was sleeping. It wasn't anything like a regular dream, though, because it was so real. I can remember it all perfectly."

"What happened? What did she say?" Micki demanded eagerly.

"Well, sometime in the middle of the night, I woke up. At least I thought I was awake. There was an incredibly bright moon shining down on my face through the window. It was nearly a full moon. I thought there was something strange about that, but it took me a while to figure out what. Then I remembered: When we went to sleep there had only been a crescent moon. I sat up like a shot and found that I wasn't in the attic at all, but in a much smaller room, which smelled of newly cut wood planks. Across from mine there was another bed. Someone was sitting on it, but it wasn't you. You can imagine what I felt when I realized who the person was."

"Her?" Micki whispered. Sarah nodded.

"Just sitting there quietly with her hands folded and that big basket beside her, like she was waiting for me to wake up. I was so frightened I couldn't speak."

"I know the feeling."

"She didn't say anything. She just stared right at me with those huge brown eyes. So I finally got up the courage to open my mouth.

"'Where is Michelle?' I asked.

"'She'll be here soon,' replied the woman.

"'Here? Where is here?'

"'Quite another time, though not another place, Sarah DeSilver.'

"'Whatever do you mean?' In answer to my question, the woman pointed to the window. The moon was streaming in, and I could see that I was on the top of a wooded hill. Below I could just make out moonlight reflected off a small lake. But I had no idea what the scene was supposed to tell me."

"You were at our cottage, of course," interrupted

Micki. "It all fits, Sarah, don't you see?" Sarah looked curiously at her cousin.

"No, Michelle, I don't in the least see. What are you talking about? What cottage?"

"Never mind." Micki waved her hand impatiently. "Go on with the story."

Sarah resumed her narrative.

"Well, I must have looked at her quite blankly, because she said 'You'll see it soon enough,' almost like she was reading my thoughts.

"'But I don't understand!' I cried.

"'Understanding is not always your strong suit, is it, chicken?' she said. 'Only when you want it to be, I suppose?' Well, it seemed such a rude thing to say to me that I suddenly found myself getting very angry, and I forgot about being frightened.

"'What business is it of yours? At least I'm not evil. At least I don't go sneaking around into other people's rooms, scaring them to death and casting horrible spells on them.' You see, I thought that would really get her—showing her that I knew about what she did to Gregory. But she didn't seem in the least bit disturbed. As a matter of fact, she smiled. It made me very uncomfortable.

"'Slow to understand, quick to judge. You've certainly given that cousin of yours the rough side of your tongue, little lady.'

"It didn't even occur to me to wonder how she

could know such a thing. All I wanted was to defend myself against her.

"'You're the one who's been telling Gregory all those dreadful things about Michelle.'

"'Dreadful things, chicken? Why, a warning is all I'm good for, and a pointing to the possible.'

"'Anyway,' I said quickly, 'I've been very decent to Michelle lately. In fact, I've rather come to like her.'

"'But you don't trust her.' When she said that, I realized it was quite true. I *didn't* trust you.

"All this time the woman hadn't moved from where she was sitting on the bed opposite me. Now she stood up slowly. She wasn't much taller standing than sitting. But she looked somehow quite terrible there by the window clutching that giant basket and shaking a finger at me.

"'It's not for you to pass judgment on her. Your cousin has certainly done wrong, but not in the way you might think—for there is much you don't know. And now she needs you, Sarah DeSilver, Riddle Solver. Much depends on your clearheadedness. Set the suspicions aside—they muddy the water. Simply listen and reflect.'

"That was all. Then the room went kind of fuzzy. It sounds strange, but it seemed like the woman was somehow going out the window. Except she wasn't moving at all. She just got farther and farther away. The last thing I remember was staring into the moon. That really made me catch my breath. Because instead of the usual man-in-the-moon pattern, what I saw was two huge brown eyes and the lines of the old woman's face. She was actually *inside* the moon!

"I don't know how I got back to my own bed, or in fact, whether I had ever really left it. But I must have gone into a very deep sleep, because I didn't wake up until quite late this morning. When I looked over and saw that your bed was empty, I suddenly panicked, though I wasn't sure why. Then I remembered my dream, and I felt I had to talk to you right away. I waited around the house for a while, but finally I got impatient and set off to find you."

"Well here I am," said Micki without much enthusiasm.

"Yes, and now I'm thinking that I've overreacted. I suppose dreaming about that old woman made me imagine things. What with Gregory—"

"How is he?" asked Micki quickly.

"No change." Sarah's voice sounded suddenly hard. The wall had gone up again, in spite of the old woman's warning advice. She looked coldly at her cousin.

"You know, Sarah," said Micki slowly, weighing her words, "the old woman was right. There's a lot you don't know. Because I haven't told you. And I haven't told you because you'd never believe me."

"Try me."

"For example, would you believe me if I told you that you're my great-great-great-aunt?"

11

Riddle Solving

The silence in the forest was so intense that a fish jumping way out in the middle of the lake sounded almost deafening. Sarah stared at her cousin blankly.

"Your *what*?" she whispered incredulously.

"I know it sounds unbelievable, but it's true. There are too many things that make it the only possible explanation."

"Explanation of what?" demanded Sarah.

"Of this whole terrible business with Gregory."

And without waiting for Sarah to question her further, Micki launched into her story. It came gushing out like a river swollen with too much spring rain. She talked and talked, giving as many details as she could remember. And though it was now getting well past noon, Sarah forgot her hunger, so engrossed was she in her cousin's tale.

"So you see," Micki concluded, "there's something I *must* do to save Gregory, because somehow I have gotten us into this mess. If only I knew what it was!" she added mournfully.

When Micki had stopped talking, Sarah said nothing for some time. The sun had grown quite warm, and she wiped away a small bead of perspiration. Finally she shook her head gravely back and forth.

"Some of it does seem to make sense. But the part about you coming to us from a future time is something that I just can't imagine. Things like that just don't happen. I'm sorry Michelle, I wish I could believe you."

Micki lowered her head in disappointment. She had so much wanted her cousin to take what she had to say on faith, no questions asked. But she had to admit, if the tables had been turned, she would have been equally doubtful of such a story.

"The thing is," said Sarah slowly, "whether all

of it is true or not doesn't really matter, does it? I mean, whenever that old woman is around, the strangest things always happen, and she makes us see what perhaps isn't actually there."

"That's true," replied Micki. "But," she added firmly, "the one thing I *do* know is where I come from, where I grew up, and who my family is."

"Very well, Michelle. If I can't believe you, I promise I won't disbelieve you either. Because now I think that's exactly what the old woman was trying to warn me against—*judging* you."

"Thank you," said Micki, much relieved.

"What I can't stop thinking about, though, is what she called me in my dream: Sarah DeSilver, Riddle Solver. It sounds very grand, doesn't it? But what does it mean? I *am* quite good at riddles, actually, but what are the riddles that need solving? Where do we start?"

"How about that strange rhyme the woman told me?" suggested Micki, and she recited it again slowly for Sarah:

*"The branch once turned to the trunk and said,
'Though it's not my wish to see you dead,
I'd so much rather we severed ties.'
But in snapping free the whole tree dies.*

"I'm pretty sure now that the 'tree' means the

family tree, and that I'm the branch," Micki explained.

"Yes, that would make sense, especially because of that game you found with our names on it," agreed Sarah. "But even if you're the branch, I'm still not sure what you could have possibly done to 'sever the tie,' as it says."

"That's just it!" Micki almost wailed. "What I'm afraid of is that just by *wishing* to be free of my family, somehow my wish has come true!"

"Well!" exclaimed Sarah. "That seems like a really dirty trick to me. I'm sure you never meant it, anyway."

"That's what I keep telling myself. But the fact is, over the past few months I had been wanting more and more to be alone, until I could hardly bear being around my family. And then this happened. Now everything feels different. But if this is called 'learning my lesson,' I'd say it's a terribly unfair way to have to do it."

"Yes, even worse than Miss Collins." Sarah grinned. "But I'm still not satisfied. I think there's something more in that rhyme than some preachy little message about loving your family. Do you know the part that stands out the most to me?"

Micki shook her head.

"That line about 'snapping free.' I mean 'snapping' is such a descriptive word, as Miss Collins might say." Sarah picked up a small branch that she had brushed aside in laying out the picnic cloth. "Why 'snapping'?" she asked, at the same time breaking the dry branch neatly in two.

Micki clenched her fists. The tingling sensation in her fingers had begun again.

"There's something I need to remember," she said quietly.

"Yes?" breathed Sarah eagerly. "Michelle, I'm sure there is. I'm sure there's something more. Think! Think back to the day you came to us—the same day as Gregory's accident. The day he fell from the tree . . ."

Micki barely heard her. She was staring at the empty space in front of her as if there were something there. She was thinking about the secret room in the toy museum and the day she had discovered the dollhouse. And the more she thought about it, the more her fingers tingled, until they were almost throbbing.

What was it that had happened there? Micki began to mentally retrace her steps from the moment she had entered the room. She forced herself to remember shouting the words she so much regretted now—"I *wish* I'd never been born!" Suddenly she gripped Sarah tightly by the wrist.

"What is it, Michelle?"

"There was a branch. A *real* branch. I snapped it. I snapped it right in half, I remember now. Just before I looked into the dollhouse that I told you about."

"And at the exact moment that huge branch snapped beneath Gregory and caused his fall," murmured Sarah.

"Yes, and don't you see I as good as killed him?" whispered Micki hoarsely. She stared at her cousin with wide, frightened eyes. "The old woman was right after all. It *is* my fault. I killed your brother!" Micki's voice had risen steadily until she sounded almost hysterical.

"Michelle!" Sarah said sharply. She shook Micki roughly by the shoulders. "Stop that this instant! You're forgetting something very important."

"What can be more important than this?"

"The fact that Gregory isn't dead yet."

"Yes, but the doctor says it's only a matter of time."

"No. Don't you remember? He said, 'Only a miracle can keep him with us now.'"

"Great. A miracle. Like a miracle is just around the corner waiting to happen."

"Michelle DeSilver! I'm surprised at you!" said Sarah reprovingly. "Don't tell me that after all that you say has happened to you, you don't believe in miracles?"

Micki was silent.

"I mean personally, I find all this business about traveling through time a lot harder to swallow than some everyday miracle," Sarah reasoned. Micki smiled at her gratefully. She knew that her cousin was as scared as she was about Gregory. Nevertheless, she was putting a very brave face on it.

"Maybe you're right," she conceded.

"Of course I'm right. But there's another thing. Why would we keep getting so many hints and warnings if there were no hope left of Gregory's recovery? And what about the old woman? If she were evil and wanted Gregory to die, I'd have thought she could have arranged it by now. So if she's not evil, why does she keep turning up all the time to speak to us about Gregory? That is, unless she's trying to tell us something?"

"Well if she's trying to tell us something, I wish she'd be more clear about it. Why can't she just come out and tell us what we're supposed to do?"

"Perhaps we're meant to discover that for ourselves," replied Sarah.

"What's the sense in that?" said Micki scornfully. It all seemed like a terrible waste of time, especially with Gregory hanging on to life by a mere thread. Sarah was thoughtful for a moment.

"Michelle, has it ever happened to you that someone tells you to do something—your parents, say—and when you ask them why, they say, 'Because I told you to'?"

"Has it ever!"

"So you don't do the thing. And then later you find out there was really a very good reason to have done it, if only you'd known at the time, or if only you'd been able figure it out for yourself before it was too late."

Micki nodded. How many times had that happened to her? It seemed as if it were at least once a day. And lately, she had to admit, it had been happening more and more. Sarah continued with her explanation.

"What I'm thinking is, perhaps the same thing is true here. Maybe we're meant to make our own discoveries—figure out *why* things are happening, and then go from there to work out what to do about them. That's why there are all these riddles and half explanations, you see. We're supposed to fill in the blanks. That way it's a lot easier to do what we have to do, if that makes any sense."

"That's all very well," replied Micki soberly. "But in the meantime, what about Gregory? While we're busy figuring all this stuff out, he might just go and die. And it will be *my* fault. *My* fault!"

"Michelle, just calm down and let me think!" said Sarah with a gesture of impatience. "No one is blaming you anymore but yourself. Not even me," she added kindly.

"Promise?" Micki asked hopefully.

"Of course."

Micki felt an immediate surge of warmth toward her cousin. It was as if Sarah had generously offered to share an enormous burden, and Micki gave up half gratefully. At the idea of burdens Micki's thoughts quickly turned to the stone egg. She glanced nervously at the two halves that still lay on the ground. They looked harmless enough.

"What about those?" she asked, nodding in their direction. Sarah followed her gaze.

"Yes, I'm wondering about that part as well. They don't seem to fit into the picture very clearly," Sarah replied, picking up one half in each hand. Micki almost hoped Sarah would see something in them, just so her own story would seem more plausible. But nothing happened.

"I don't think there's much else we can do right now, so we might as well enjoy our picnic," said Sarah in a practical tone, planting the stones firmly on diagonal corners of the picnic cloth to weigh it down against the breeze.

Micki sighed. It was wonderful to have someone else to do some of the thinking and the worrying. Suddenly she realized she was ravenously hungry after all. She smiled at Sarah, who was wistfully eyeing a golden-crusted meat pie, and as if they were of a single mind, the girls each reached for a fork and fell on the food like starving animals. To Micki it was the most delicious picnic food she had ever tasted.

"Have you chosen your saying yet, Michelle?" asked Aunt Lydia, reaching into her workbasket for Micki's sampler. Sarah and Mary had gone off to call on some neighbors, so Micki and her aunt were alone in the sitting room.

Now that she had nearly completed the letters of the alphabet, Aunt Lydia reminded her, it was time to start planning the more challenging part of her assignment. Two days had passed since the picnic in the forest, but to Micki it seemed like an age since she had last plied her needle. She fervently hoped she had not forgotten how. Certainly the furthest thing from her mind of late had been coming up with the kind of preachy saying one might safely put on a sampler.

Micki lowered her head and closed her eyes. If only she could remember some bit of recitation from Miss Collins, she would be able to produce a phrase that would please her aunt. But it was hopeless. The unpleasant teacher's instruction had been totally erased from her mind.

"I haven't quite decided yet," Micki stalled.

"Why Michelle, what on earth have you done to

it?" Aunt Lydia was gazing, tight-lipped, at the material that lay in her lap. "I would hardly call this an appropriate selection for a sampler. I can't think what you meant by it," she said severely, handing the piece of work to her niece. Micki noticed that her hand was trembling slightly.

Micki took it and stared. There, traced neatly on her sampler beneath the nearly completed alphabet, were five lines of what looked like a short poem:

> *Sticks and stones will break his bones*
> *And hope is all in vain*
> *When stick meets stone*
> *A wish alone*
> *Will make him whole again*

"I'm sorry, Aunt Lydia. I guess it's just something I learned somewhere." The lie was out almost before she knew she had said it.

"Well, what's done is done," replied her aunt. She seemed to have regained some of her composure. "And now that you've gone and traced it, you'll have to stitch the whole thing in. It's rather more than I would have recommended for a first sampler," she added, with a wry smile.

Micki's mind was racing, but she was careful to concentrate on her sewing so that her aunt would not see how much she, too, had been disturbed by this latest development. She was certain that the writing on the sampler was a message meant for her. It seemed to be some kind of riddle, but she had only a vague inkling of its meaning. Suddenly she thought of her cousin and the name the old woman had given her—Sarah DeSilver, Riddle Solver.

"Aunt Lydia, when is Sarah coming back? I have to talk to her," she said impulsively.

"Any minute now, I expect," replied her aunt. "Michelle, is there anything wrong?"

"Oh, no," said Micki quickly. "I just forgot to tell her something." She looked away from her aunt's penetrating gaze, trying hard to think of some bit of casual conversation. It was with relief that she heard Sarah's voice in the hallway announcing the sisters' return. Micki rose with a start.

"Michelle, what letter are you on?" asked Aunt Lydia sternly.

"I'm just finishing up the Y," she replied, smoothing out her work to survey her progress. Was it her imagination or had the lettering of the phrase at the bottom become darker?

"In that case, you're far too close to the end to stop now," replied Aunt Lydia with a wicked twinkle in her eye. "Since you seem to be so eager to speak to Sarah, I'll just have to call her in here to sit and sew with us for a while."

Helplessly Micki watched as Sarah and Mary were ushered into the sitting room and set to work on their respective projects. She didn't dare look Sarah in the eye with Aunt Lydia watching them so closely. Instead she turned her attention back to her sewing, determined to finish the alphabet as quickly as possible so she would be free to go.

"Finished!" she announced at last, biting off the thread with her teeth triumphantly.

"Someone *is* in a hurry," declared Aunt Lydia. "Let me have a look."

Micki hesitated. She was reluctant to let the sampler out of her hands, but saw she had no choice.

"Mmm," said Aunt Lydia, examining Micki's handiwork with a critical eye. "Rushing never pays, Michelle. Look here how sloppy you've become. I'm afraid you're going to have to rip out the last two letters and begin again."

"Aunt Lydia," said Micki slowly, "I promise I'll do it over, but may I *please* do it upstairs in our room?" Immediately Sarah caught the agitation in her voice and looked up in concern. Their eyes met, and Micki uttered a silent prayer that her cousin would think of some means to get her mother to release them.

Sarah did not disappoint her. She laid down her sewing and said, "Michelle, how is your head this afternoon?"

"My what?"

"You know, that awful headache you woke up with this morning. Is it any better now?"

"Oh. Yes, a bit." Micki fumbled and saw her cousin frown. "But it seems to be coming back again after all this sewing," she added quickly.

"Michelle, why didn't you tell me you weren't feeling well?" cried Aunt Lydia in alarm. "You must march up to bed right away. Sarah can rip these last two letters out for you," she added, handing the sampler to her daughter. And before Aunt Lydia could say anything further, the two cousins were bounding up the stairs to their attic room, taking two steps at a time and completely forgetting that Micki was supposed to be suffering from a terrible headache.

"What can it possibly mean?" whispered Micki. The two of them were alone in the attic with the sampler spread out on Sarah's bed. All the same, they were whispering as though at any moment someone might decide to creep upstairs and listen at the keyhole.

"I should think it was fairly obvious," said Sarah with an air of importance. She was relishing her

161

role as Riddle Solver.

"Well?" demanded Micki impatiently.

"The stone must be your stone egg."

"That much I got—what about the stick?"

"The stick must be the stick that you broke," replied Sarah. "When the stick meets the stone, he, meaning Gregory, will get well again."

"But that's impossible!" cried Micki. "How can the stick meet the stone when that stick is up in some old museum that I can't get to from here? Mostly because it's a hundred years away?"

Sarah shook her head doubtfully. "I don't know about that. All I know is we have to get that stick—it's the only way we can save him. Don't you see? We're *meant* to get it!"

"You mean *I'm* meant to," grumbled Micki. "You don't even believe it is where it is."

Sarah looked troubled. "What would be the best way to go about it?" she asked gingerly.

"Well," replied Micki with sarcasm, "first I'd have to get back to my own time. But right now my family is at the lake for our vacation. So I'd have to convince them that we had to go home. *Then* I'd have to beg them to take me back to the toy museum, which is probably the last place they'd want to go. Once I got them there, I'd have to slip away and try to find that room again—the one that was marked 'PRIVATE.' And all of this is assuming that the stick is still there and hasn't been swept up and taken out with a load of rubbish."

"Maybe you won't have to do all that. Maybe you'll just end up where you're supposed to be." It was an appealing thought. Micki wished she could just open a door, step into the secret room, find that miserable branch, bring it back, and have done with the whole episode. But somehow she didn't think it would be so simple.

"That's easy for you to say," she said in an irritated tone. "You're not the one who has to go through with it."

"Well it's not my fault in the first place," replied Sarah hotly. "You said yourself it was you that got Gregory into this mess."

To Micki her cousin's cruel words were like a slap in the face. Tears of hurt sprang to her eyes and she opened her mouth to respond, but no words came. Sarah looked at her somewhat guiltily, then pursed her lips in stubborn defiance and turned away toward the window.

Micki stood up. Feeling suddenly as friendless as when she had first come to the house, her immediate thought was to get away at once, and she ran blindly from the room before Sarah had a chance to shout for her to wait. Down the attic stairs she ran, down another flight, past the room

163

where Aunt Lydia and Mary still sat sewing and murmuring in low voices, past the dining room where the servants were laying the table for the midday meal, into the front hallway, and out the door into the open air of the gray afternoon.

Instinctively, Micki headed for the woods and the lake that had been the scene of so many strange events and encounters. Somehow she sensed that whatever was going to happen next would have to happen there.

It almost seemed as if the woods themselves were making way for her as she ran. Nothing as obvious as trees moving aside or branches parting. Rather there was something about the air itself. Not only was it growing warmer, it also had a shimmering quality, like rippling water. But it wasn't until Micki heard her sister's voice calling her in the distance that she realized she was actually running through time.

12

Retracing Steps

When she reached the clearing by the lake, breathless but otherwise showing no sign of the tears and upset she had felt only moments earlier, Micki found her family assembled at the dock, readying their rowboat for its first fishing trip of the season. She had surprisingly little trouble explaining her whereabouts and realized that not enough time had elapsed for anyone to start worrying. In fact, it seemed they had all just arrived.

Jenny was delighted to see her and immediately

launched into a description of the trip with their father to the tackle shop. Micki smiled. She suddenly felt as if her worries could wait. Right now she just wanted to enjoy this beautiful spring day, even if it meant having to listen to her sister's chattering the whole way through.

"It's perfect," she murmured to herself, gazing up at the azure sky. "I don't think *anything* can spoil it."

She was right. The day unfolded before them like a gift wrapped in blue-and-gold paper. Their father took them out in the boat, and as soon as the little craft had drifted some distance from the shore an awesome quiet descended on them, broken only by the dipping of the oars and an occasional jumping fish. Even Jenny was affected by the powerful silence, and she became almost contemplative, contenting herself with now and then lowering her hand into the glasslike smoothness of the water and watching as the little ripples spread out in ever-widening circles from the boat.

In the morning they caught no fish, but they finally returned, ravenously hungry, to the shore and the picnic Mrs. Silver had laid out for them. It wasn't until she had seated herself comfortably with a plate of food in her lap that Micki was reminded of that other happy picnic she had shared with her cousin just two days ago. But she quickly pushed all thoughts of Sarah from her mind.

After the picnic they sat about lazily talking and laughing. Micki's mother brought out her embroidery and began stitching in the floral pattern. But she was only half concentrating and soon threw the work down in frustration. Micki picked it up and examined it with interest. The design was far less complicated than anything she'd seen at the DeSilvers', and without thinking she began sewing where her mother had left off.

"My oh my!" her mother breathed. She was staring at her daughter in amazement. Micki flushed and quickly handed the work back to her mother, who inspected it and slowly shook her head.

"Why Micki, I almost can't tell your stitches from mine. Wherever did my little tomboy learn to embroider like that?"

"Oh, in school," replied Micki carelessly. She was thinking it would have been nice if Aunt Lydia felt the same way as her mother about her needlework.

"Really? I wasn't aware they still taught sewing in the schools," her father joined in. "I hope they teach the boys as well. It's a valuable skill to have."

"It may be a valuable skill," his wife said, smiling, "but I happen to know they *don't* teach it at Micki's school."

"I *did* learn it at school," Micki insisted. "From a friend."

"And who might this talented friend be?" asked her father with interest.

"Her name is Sarah. She's very clever. She plays the piano as well."

And almost as though she were trying to make it up to her cousin for leaving her in such an angry rush, Micki began to embellish the description of Sarah with so many interesting details that her mother finally said, "Micki Silver, I can't imagine why you haven't invited this wonderful Sarah over to our house. As soon as the new trimester starts, I'll call her mother and ask if Sarah can spend the weekend with us."

Micki stared at her mother in dismay. Now she'd done it. She'd gone and said too much and her parents were sure to keep asking about Sarah and wondering why she never brought her home. She wouldn't be surprised if her mother made inquiries at the school, and after that she'd really be in hot water. They'd think she made the whole thing up.

"I can't ask her."

"Why not, sweetheart?"

"Her family is moving away. Soon. Next week," she added quickly.

"What a shame," said Mrs. Silver. She looked at

her daughter with a quizzical expression but said nothing more.

Both Micki and Jenny had enjoyed the boat excursion so much that they begged their father to take them out again. This time their fishing proved more successful. It was Jenny who felt the first bite, and she nearly dropped the fishing rod in her excitement. In a moment Mr. Silver was at her side, and together they landed a long hefty-looking fish.

The animal slapped about furiously in the bottom of the boat, its silvery sides flashing in the sunlight like a coat of jewels. Jenny squealed in terror.

"Perch," said Mr. Silver with satisfaction. "That's dinner for tonight."

"Yuck!" cried Micki and Jenny in unison. Micki looked at the struggling animal with a mixture of pity and disgust. The last thing she wanted was to have it for dinner. But suddenly she felt a tugging on her own fishing rod and all was forgotten in the excitement of bringing in her first catch. It wasn't long before her father, too, had landed a fish—a beautiful striped bass. Within an hour Mr. Silver had to call a halt to the fishing. It was wasteful, he said, to catch fish they didn't plan to eat. So the rest of the day was spent lazing about on the water and exploring the nearby inlets and surrounding woods.

By the time the family returned from the lake, it was already getting dark. A flush of pink clouds shone like fluorescent cotton candy through the trees behind the cottage. Below, toward the lake, the somber gray that had settled over the water had begun its slow creep up the hill. The air had turned crisp with cold. There was a single light on in the house, but it made the place look warm and inviting.

Halfway up the hill they heard a faint ringing noise coming from the cottage. It sounded strangely insistent out there in the middle of the unspoiled forest.

"Drat that noise, it's the telephone!" exclaimed Mr. Silver. "Why is someone bothering us all the way out here?" In spite of his irritation at being disturbed, he ran the rest of the way to the house, and the family could see him through the window dropping his gear and making a dash for the phone. When they got inside, Mr. Silver's exasperated voice sounded from the living room.

"Jack, please, can't this wait a week? I'm on holiday with the family. It's the kids' spring vacation."

Micki and her mother looked at each other in dismay. Jack was her father's boss. He rarely called Mr. Silver at home, but when he did, it invariably meant trouble at the office. The fact that he was calling him all the way out here meant extra-special trouble.

"All right, all right," Mr. Silver was saying. "How long do you think it will take? Okay . . . Yes . . . If I catch a flight back early in the morning, I can be in the office by noon. Yeah, I'm sorry too." He hung up the phone and looked around at his woebegone family. They already knew what was coming next.

"I'm really sorry, honey," he said, appealing to his wife for support. "But there's nothing I can do about it. Apparently something went wrong with the computer, and everything for next week's presentation was lost. Now we've all got to get together and try to reconstruct the whole thing from memory and rough drafts."

"How long will it take?" asked Mrs. Silver quietly.

"We ought to be able to get it done in a day or two if we really put our minds to it. In any event, Jack says I can be back here by Thursday evening or Friday morning at the very latest."

"Well, if you must, you must," his wife replied with resignation. "The girls and I will be fine."

But Micki had no doubt that this glitch in the family's vacation plans was no mere coincidence. To her it was a sign as clear as day that she had to be on that flight home with her father. The question was how to manage it. Suddenly the weight of her task returned to her, and she longed for Sarah's resourcefulness.

"Well, we might as well fry up some of these fish for supper," said Mr. Silver in an attempt to be cheerful. But the mood of the day had been broken. Jenny began to whimper that she was cold, and her mother took her upstairs for a warm bath.

Micki and her father were alone for the first time since they had both realized the truth about the lake. There was a strained silence until Micki, who had given up the idea of trying to be subtle, blurted out, "Daddy, I have to go with you. I have to go back to the toy museum."

Instead of protesting he simply looked at her briefly and murmured, "Yes, I knew there was something about that place the moment I set foot in it. It's that house, isn't it, Micki? The one that was up in the attic."

Micki nodded. "Yes. I'm sure I left something there. Something important."

Her father shook his head. "Micki, I don't know what you're up to, but I'm going to trust you on this one. For some reason I feel as if you know what you're doing. So I'll tell you what: I'll think of something to tell your mother about why you should come with me."

He pondered for a moment, and then snapped his fingers.

"I've got it! We'll say you didn't have a chance to say good-bye to your friend Sarah. In fact, we can even go around to her house and do just that!"

Mr. Silver was so pleased with this clever plan that he failed to notice his daughter's disturbed expression. But Micki thought it best to say nothing further about Sarah. Perhaps when they got home and her father got involved with his work, he would forget all about the intended visit. In the meantime, everything seemed to be moving so smoothly that she was almost worried. Surely some trap was waiting for her—some challenge she would have to face so that her task could be accomplished.

The trip back was uneventful, except for the excitement of the airplane ride. Micki had been in a plane only once before and that was several years ago. It had been a very large plane, and she hardly noticed they were flying once they got off the ground. This time it was different.

The nearest airport to the lake was a small rural affair with one runway that only serviced tiny propeller planes. The plane they were flying in had just twenty seats, and even Micki had to bend down to get through the doorway. Micki sat in the window seat and watched eagerly as the engine started up and the propellers began whirring noisily until they were a whitish blur.

When they finally took off, Micki clutched her armrests in terror as the plane bumped and coughed its way up through the cloud cover like an antique motor car. But her father assured her that all small planes were like this—she might as well relax and enjoy the ride. So Micki pretended she was at an amusement park and squealed in delight each time the plane dipped with a crosswind.

She'd barely had time to finish her glass of orange juice when the captain announced they were ready to land. Before Micki knew it, she and her father were speeding toward home in a rental car. It seemed unbelievable, after yesterday's endless car ride, that they could be back so quickly.

How Mr. Silver had convinced his wife to let Micki accompany him Micki would never know. She had her doubts that her mother bought the story about saying good-bye to Sarah. But somehow it had all been arranged. Micki was to stay with their next-door neighbor during the day until her father arrived home in the evening. But today he had promised to take her to the toy museum before he reported for work. Only they'd have to hurry. He needed to get everything done as quickly as possible so they could be back at the lake in two days.

Mr. Silver had no trouble finding the toy museum this time. In fact, though it had not occurred to him earlier, the museum was actually only a five-minute walk from his office. On a sunny day both the street and the building that housed the museum looked far less ominous, and Micki felt almost lighthearted as they began climbing the stairs. But when they finally reached the top landing, she was seized with a sudden reluctance, and she stood behind her father as he pounded on the door to be let in. It swung open immediately, almost as if someone had been waiting for them.

Micki was expecting to be greeted by the mysterious old proprietress with the penetrating eyes, but the woman who stood in the doorway couldn't have been more different. She was enormously tall, and her straggly brown hair was piled in a sloppy bun on top of her head, making her look even taller. She had a very broad pale face, and she stared at Mr. Silver with equally pale blue eyes. She looked vaguely apologetic.

"I'm afraid it's Wednesday today," the woman murmured with apparent irrelevance.

"Yes, I'm afraid it is," replied Micki's father, sighing in mock sympathy. He gave his daughter a wink.

"Well, as you can see from the sign, we're closed today." Micki's heart fell, and she let out a wail of dismay. The woman looked startled and appeared to see her for the first time.

"Closed to *adults*, that is. The little girl can come in, of course. Wednesday is our children-only day."

Mr. Silver was examining the sign. It seemed to have been newly painted since the last time they had been there, and it clearly read: "Wednesdays—Children Only."

Micki eyed her father anxiously as he shook his head.

"I think I could write a book on the entrance rules for this place," he commented dryly. "Well, Micki, it seems a shame to come all this way and then not go in. I'll tell you what. You stay and enjoy yourself. I'll just nip over to the office and come back for you in an hour's time. How's that?"

Micki smiled nervously. That would suit her just fine, she told him. She had been wondering how she'd be able to give her father the slip once they got inside. At the same time she was almost hoping that it wouldn't be possible. Then she could at least say she'd tried.

"So what are the financial arrangements today?" he asked the woman with a touch of irony in his voice. "Are we good or are we bad?"

She gave him a blank stare and replied, "Fifty cents, the same as always."

Mr. Silver paid her and, patting Micki fondly on the cheek, turned and left.

The woman ushered her into the huge reception room of the museum and promptly wandered off, leaving Micki alone. She took a deep breath.

"No more excuses, I guess," she said aloud, as if giving encouragement to someone else.

Micki thought she would surely have trouble finding the room again, especially since she had only discovered it after running blindly through the endless chambers of the museum. But as soon as she began walking, she seemed to know instinctively which way to turn. She moved through the rooms as if in a trance, hardly noticing the limitless display of toys that surrounded her, until she reached her destination—the door marked "PRIVATE."

Micki's hand trembled on the doorknob. The last time she had barged in without thinking, but now she hesitated. What if everything was not as she had left it? Then all would have been in vain. Squeezing her eyes tight and making a secret wish, Micki pushed open the door.

When she opened her eyes, all she could see were some vague shapes in the recesses of the room. The oval window admitted the gray light of a damp, gloomy day. Nothing like the glorious sunshine of just a few moments ago. More like the depressing weather she had left behind her in the nineteenth century.

Micki closed the door and took a few steps toward the center of the room. From a far corner came a faint creaking noise. She stood very still, letting her eyes become accustomed to the partial darkness. The creaking sounded again. Micki drew closer, her heart pounding violently.

"Well done," said a deep voice. Seated in an old rocking chair, her feet barely touching the ground, was the ancient proprietress of the museum. Her deep brown eyes stared calmly at Micki in the dim light.

Seeing her once again, Micki had the same reaction as her father: There was something about the woman that made Micki sure that she and the Egg Lady were one and the same. The funny thing was, as her father had said, they didn't really *look* the same, even though they were both very small and very old. And they certainly didn't sound the same. The proprietress's voice was far deeper than the Egg Lady's. But there was no mistaking the strength of that gaze.

Suddenly Micki noticed that the woman's gnarled fingers were resting on an object that lay in her lap. Tremulously, she drew closer. It was a broken branch.

"Yes, it's here, the product of the ill-fated deed," the woman said in what sounded almost like a mocking tone.

"I'm to bring it back." It was half a demand and half a question.

"You wish now to undo your wish?"

"Yes, of course," said Micki impatiently. The woman continued her unbroken stare.

"Why me?" Micki demanded in an angry tone. "Plenty of people make silly wishes when they're upset. That doesn't mean they really want them to come true. And what's more, they don't."

"Perhaps they don't make those wishes in magic rooms marked 'PRIVATE,'" replied the old woman tartly.

Micki was silent. Her eyes were now accustomed to the light, and for the first time she noticed the dollhouse at the the far corner of the room, in the exact spot where she had first seen it. The woman followed her gaze.

"Go ahead. Yes, they're in there."

Cautiously, Micki crept closer until she was able to peer down into the attic bedroom. Once again the room was alive. Sarah was seated on her bed, with her hands folded. She looked extremely frightened.

"Oh Michelle, where *have* you gone?" she said aloud. She stood up and began pacing back and forth across the room, nervously twirling one of her long braids. She turned around eagerly when the door opened behind her. Her face fell when she saw it was Mary. Mary's face was very white.

"Sarah, Dr. Bain says it's only a matter of hours now. They're allowing each of us to say good-bye to him. You're to come down in half an hour." Without another word, Mary turned and left.

For a moment Sarah simply stared blankly at the doorway where Mary had been standing. Then she let out a piteous wail.

"NO! He *can't* die!" Frantically, she ran to the window. "Michelle! I'm sorry! *Please* come back!"

Micki whirled around to face the old woman. "After all this, and now he's going to die anyway?" she cried in an accusatory tone.

"That's up to you," was the reply.

"But there's no *time*," Micki fairly shouted.

"Time is a funny thing. Surely you know that by now."

"Why can't I just go back now, from here, instead of going all the way back to the lake?" Micki insisted. "I'm sure you could send me there now if you wanted to."

"You can send yourself. You're in a wishing room, after all. You've only to make the wish and go." The old woman gestured toward the door of the dollhouse.

"Why didn't you say so before!" Micki exclaimed. Perhaps things weren't so bleak after all. She turned toward the dollhouse and placed her hands over her eyes so she could concentrate on making her wish.

"Of course, getting *back* is quite another matter."

Micki drew in her breath sharply. She stopped midwish.

"What do you mean?"

"I mean you get only one wish. Wishing yourself back won't do any good."

"I've come back before," said Micki, puzzled.

"Not from here. There are all kinds of wishing places. In this room you may receive one wish each time you enter. Haven't you noticed that you always return from the past to the exact moment that you left in the present?"

Micki nodded.

"That's because part of you is really still here. If you wish to go to the past from here, you'd actually remain here in the present, with your one wish used up, and nothing in the world could bring you back to the present."

Micki clenched her fists in exasperation. Why was everything so complicated, when all she really

181

wanted to do was make sure Gregory got well again?

"Of course, you can still return the long way—from the lake, the way you came." Micki was about to protest once more that Gregory might die in the meantime, but she remembered what the old woman had said about time being a funny thing.

"Then you'll give me the branch?" she asked timidly.

"Ah, the branch! You know you almost returned without it?"

Micki clapped her hand over her mouth. So she had! What a fool she would have looked! And how could she have faced Sarah, returning empty-handed? She shuddered at the thought.

The old woman began wrapping the branch in a piece of material that lay in her lap. She held it up to Micki. As Micki reached to take it, their eyes met.

"You still have one wish, you know."

Micki was silent.

"Perhaps you'd like a piece of advice?"

"Please."

"Don't simply wish for the first thing that comes into your head. That's never wise in a wishing room, you know. Choose *efficiently*."

Efficiently. What a strange word to use when

talking about wishes, Micki mused. Of course, the first thing that came into her head was for Gregory to be made well again. But then a thought occurred to her. If she wished for something in her own future, it would mean that Gregory would have to get well in order for her wish to come true. Perhaps that was what the old woman meant by "wishing efficiently."

And suddenly it seemed only right to Micki that she should return to the DeSilvers and see her task through to the end, even if it meant taking the time and the energy to go back the long way. So Micki decided to wish for something entirely unrelated to Gregory.

She took a deep breath, looked straight into the old woman's eyes, and said firmly, "What I really and truly wish for is to be able to finish the rest of my holiday at the lake with my family."

For the first time the old woman smiled. It was a very warm smile.

"You have chosen wisely, Michelle Ann Silver," she said.

Then everything happened so quickly, Micki felt as if she were running on automatic pilot. The old woman gave her the branch, and she stowed it solemnly inside her windbreaker. When she returned to the main entrance of the museum, her father was waiting for her impatiently. But he was all smiles.

"You'll never guess what's happened, kitten!" he said gaily. Micki held her breath, not knowing what to expect.

"It was all a false alarm. They got the computer working again, and managed to find everything they lost. That means if we hurry we can get right back on the plane and be at the lake in time for dinner. I'm sorry, but we won't have a chance to look up your friend Sarah."

"That's okay, Daddy," Micki said quickly, smiling secretly at her narrow escape.

On the way back they hardly spoke, and Micki noticed that her father studiously avoided asking her anything about her visit to the museum. Her mother and Jenny met them at the airport.

"Thank goodness you're back," said her mother smilingly. "Jenny's been moping about all day wondering what on earth to do without you."

Micki was longing to ask her father to take them out on the boat again before dinner. But she knew in her heart that the rest of their holiday hung in a balance, and the sooner she did what she had to do, the better for all of them.

13

The Cure

Now that Micki was so close to the end of her task, she was eager to complete it. At the same time, she felt a strong reluctance to return to the nineteenth century. She knew what was troubling her. She was having doubts. If it were true that it would be impossible for her to return to her own time in one instance, she reasoned, what was to say that she would be able to get back this time at all?

Nevertheless, as soon as she was able to slip away, Micki headed for the lake. She stood in the little glen clutching the branch and waiting impatiently as the afternoon drew on. Any moment she was expecting that strange fading, fuzzy sensation that came when she shifted times. But her surroundings remained as crisp and clear as ever.

"I wish I could just *make* it happen if it has to happen, instead of waiting about in this way," she muttered testily.

When she heard the familiar rustling in the undergrowth behind her, her immediate thought was that she had succeeded in changing times on command after all. And indeed, when she looked around, it was Sarah who stood before her. But she stared at her cousin in disbelief. For this was not the girl in the starched pinafore whom she had come to know so well, but a proper tomboy in a T-shirt and dirty jeans.

Sarah appeared as bewildered as Micki. She gazed about her at the trees and the lake, and then at her clothing, which she fingered in amazement. Her eyes were very red, and it looked as though she'd either been crying or just been through a sandstorm.

"This time it looks like you're the one who's jumped times," said Micki, once she had recovered from her surprise.

"Everything looks somehow different," whispered Sarah, looking around her.

"Yes, trees can grow quite a bit in a hundred years."

"And these clothes . . ."

"Much nicer, aren't they?" Micki smiled. "Far more comfortable. I mean, try taking a deep breath. Then touch your toes. Then run around a little, or try climbing up that tree over there."

Micki began hopping back and forth to demonstrate. For a moment she forgot the seriousness of their situation, and Sarah giggled and followed suit. Soon the two of them were shouting in excitement and tearing wildly about the glen in pursuit of one another. When they could run no more, they collapsed breathless and laughing at the foot of the giant pine tree.

"I do believe you're right," gasped Sarah. "But is this really a hundred years from now?"

"Yes. Or your time is a hundred years ago, depending on how you look at it."

The two cousins said nothing for some time. They lay on their backs staring up at the chinks of blue sky that filtered down through the tree branches. Suddenly Sarah sat bolt upright. Micki stirred uneasily.

"Michelle, I saw her again."

"When? What did she say?" she asked expectantly. Micki was hoping for some kind of sign or instruction.

"It was just now, on my way into the forest. I'd come out to look for you. To tell you that Gregory is dying."

"I know," said Micki sadly. "I'll explain later," she added quickly when she saw her cousin's questioning look.

"I couldn't have been walking for more than five minutes when I heard a noise. I was sure it was you, so I started running toward it, calling out to you at the same time. I ran right by her. I thought she was a tree, she was standing so still. But suddenly a hand reached out to stop me as I ran past. Goodness, did I scream."

Micki shuddered.

"'Looking for someone, chicken?' she asked. I didn't want to tell her anything, so I kept my mouth shut.

"'Your little cousin, perhaps?' It's creepy the way she seems to get inside your mind. It was silly of me, but I tried to bluff her.

"'I couldn't care less where Michelle is. I'm taking a walk by myself,' I replied. I knew right away I never should have said it.

"'Aren't we the saucy one today! The pair of you are like peas in a pod. Less spice and more sugar's what you both need. But don't you think you *ought* to care where your cousin is, chicken?'

"'Why should I?'

"'Because she's been gone from here for two whole days, and time is running out. And now that she's ready to return, she needs your help.' When she said that, I had this horrible sinking sensation.

"'Oh dear, but what can *I* possibly do to help?' I was pleading with her, hoping she wouldn't say what I was afraid she was about to. But sure enough, she said, 'You must bring her back yourself.'

"'How can I bring her back if I don't know where she's gone?' But in my heart of hearts I did know.

"'She's gone to the place you don't believe in— but it's time you did.' The idea of going somewhere in another time sounded very unappealing to me. The one thing that wouldn't stop running through my mind was—what if I can't get back? Then I won't have done anyone any good, especially Gregory.

"'But Michelle's always managed to get back before. Can't she just do the same thing again this time?' I asked. I was really getting terrified, and I kept thinking, If only there were some other way.

"'Unfortunately not. Your cousin is having doubts. And doubts can destroy the strongest of wills.'

"'But what if I can't get back?' I finally demanded. I had to know.

"'Don't you think your cousin has had that very thought herself?' Suddenly I felt like such a selfish beast, I could have hit myself. Here I was, worrying only about myself, and Gregory was dying and you were in trouble.

"'I'll go this very instant!' I said to the woman. But she must have seen how scared I was, because she looked at me and said, 'You've been there once before, you know.' I knew she was talking about my dream, and that made me feel a lot better.

"'What must I do?' I asked impatiently. Now that I'd made up my mind, I couldn't wait to find you.

"'A wish is a powerful thing, chicken. You're as good as there already. Now go follow that nose of yours.'

"And without another word, she reached into her basket and pulled out a handful of something that she threw right in my face. At first I thought it was dirt or sand, but it was too fine. It smelled like . . . it's hard to describe what it smelled like. Sort of like flowers, sort of like earth, a little like pine needles. If I had to choose one word, I suppose I'd say it smelled like springtime—only ten times stronger than when you simply step out the door and breathe in the spring air.

"Anyway, it made me sneeze quite violently, and my eyes started to water. I guess I can only take so much springtime all rolled up into one. I sneezed so much that I began to feel dizzy, and my head started throbbing like it might explode. In fact, everything around me seemed to be expanding. Then all of a sudden it stopped and I stepped into the glen dressed like this and saw you standing there."

Neither girl spoke once Sarah had concluded her story.

"By the way," said Sarah finally, "I think I owe you an apology."

"What for?"

"For not believing you. I think that's one of the reasons I'm here."

"I wouldn't have believed me, either," replied Micki somewhat brusquely. Accepting apologies embarrassed her as much as making them, and she wanted to change the subject as quickly as possible.

"So what do we do now? I have the branch," she said, drawing it out carefully from inside her windbreaker. "But we're here, and he's there."

"Somehow I don't think it will be that difficult to get back now that we're together," said Sarah, holding out a hand to Micki. And she was right.

It seemed strange that Sarah should have to come forward one hundred years just to spend ten minutes in the woods wearing blue jeans. But

Micki realized later that without her cousin's help, she would never have had the will to return. And now that Sarah knew Micki had been telling the truth all along, she set her sights on their task with renewed conviction.

Whatever the reason, as soon as Sarah touched her hand Micki knew they were traveling back again. When she tried to speak and reassure her cousin, her voice made the strangest noise, almost as if she were underwater. It was the sound of her words bouncing back through the years.

"Well," said Sarah, smiling and glancing down ruefully. "I do wish we could have kept those clothes." Micki stood up and straightened her pinafore. Then she noticed the branch that she continued to clutch tightly in her left hand.

"Why, it's come whole again!" she exclaimed.

"Surely that's a hopeful sign!" cried Sarah excitedly. "Come on—now that we're back, the clock is ticking. We've no time to lose!" Together the girls tore off through the woods and back across the meadow to the house.

When they arrived home, breathless and flushed from the effort of running, they both looked the picture of health. Anyone would have thought they'd just returned from a joyful afternoon romp, and when Mary greeted them at the door, that was evidently her impression.

"Oh, Sarah, how *could* you run off to play, with Gregory the way he is?" Mary was close to tears. "We've been looking all over for you. You're to go to him at once. He's fading very fast."

Micki and Sarah exchanged glances. It was obviously useless to attempt an explanation. Besides, it would take too much time. With heavy steps they went upstairs, Sarah to Gregory's bedroom, Micki to fetch the stone egg from the attic. It had suddenly occurred to both of them that they had no idea what to do next. But they knew that whatever it was, it was their only chance.

When Micki looked down at Gregory's pale face, she was sure it was already too late. Sarah was alone in the room. Somehow she had managed to get rid of everyone, even the new nurse.

"He's still breathing," Sarah said in answer to Micki's terrified expression. "Have you brought everything?" Micki nodded. She laid the branch and the two halves of the stone egg gingerly on the bed. Then she drew out the mysterious sampler and unrolled it so they could read the message once more.

"When stick meets stone," read Sarah aloud. "Well it certainly seems clear enough. Perhaps you should do it, since you—"

"All right, all right," said Micki quickly. She

knew Sarah was about to say "since you started it," and she didn't want to hear it. She sighed heavily and looked once again at Gregory. His thin white hands lay motionless on the dark quilt. Tremulously, Micki placed one half of the stone in each of Gregory's hands. She shuddered to feel how icy cold they were. She pressed his palms together around the stone.

"Here goes," she said, lifting the branch and positioning it so that it rested lightly between Gregory's fingers, just touching the stone. Both girls held their breath.

But nothing happened.

Sarah stared at Micki with a mixture of disappointment and terror. Could it all have been a lot of silly nonsense after all?

"What have we done wrong?" wailed Micki. Sarah snatched up the sampler as if it might hold the clue to their failure.

"When stick meets stone, a wish alone," she repeated. "Michelle, have you made a wish?"

Micki gasped. She'd completely forgotten. She closed her eyes to concentrate, but too many thoughts were running through her mind.

What if Gregory died? What would happen to her? What would it feel like to become unborn? Would it hurt or would she simply disappear? Then a thought came to her: If Gregory died, *noth-*

ing would happen to her. She would simply stay right where she was. As Michelle DeSilver of the nineteenth century. It was the rest of her family—her father and Jenny—and Micki Silver who would never be born.

She hesitated. Would that be so bad? After all, she could stay here with Sarah—Sarah, a better friend than she'd ever had. She conjured up an image of the two of them spending the summer days by the lake and the evenings up in the attic room, laughing and sharing secrets.

"Gregory, please don't die!" whimpered a frightened voice. Micki opened her eyes to see Sarah kneeling by the bed and staring with a panicked expression into her brother's ghostly features. Suddenly Micki thought of her sister and the look of joy on her face when she had stepped off the airplane that afternoon.

"Micki Silver," she said to herself, "sometimes you are the biggest fool!" And moving closer to Sarah she said in a loud, clear voice, "Gregory, please *live!*"

This time there was no mistaking that something was taking place. A low humming noise had begun to fill the room. It seemed to emanate from the walls, and then come closer until the whole bed was surrounded by a sound like that of hundreds of bees busily gathering honey.

"Look! It's glowing!" cried Sarah excitedly, pointing to Gregory's clasped hands. Sure enough, the stone egg had turned a soft golden color, and it shone through Gregory's pale fingers like a miniature sun. And as it continued to glow, it seemed to spread warmth through his body. For where before his cheeks had been a dreadful ashen color, now there was a faint spot of red in the center of each.

Then something very strange happened. The branch, which had been lying across Gregory's legs, just touching the stone egg, began to tremble, just ever so slightly. And with each tiny movement, it seemed to grow fainter and fainter, until it was a mere outline that faded into nothingness. At the same moment, the humming stopped and the room became very still. But it was no longer the stillness of death. It was the stillness of breathless expectancy.

Neither girl dared to move. Suddenly a loud noise made them both start violently. Gregory had tossed his arm to one side, causing the stone egg to fall to the floor with a thud. Micki picked it up quickly. It was whole. There was no sign of the split.

"Gregory!" cried Sarah, flinging her arms across her brother's chest. Slowly he opened his eyes. With a confused expression he gazed about the room and then back to Sarah.

"Sarah! I've been having the most peculiar and horrible dreams. Something about a tree. I must have been asleep for hours." He yawned luxuriously.

"Mama, Mama, come quick!" yelled Sarah, rushing to the bedroom door. Aunt Lydia came running down the corridor with the rest of the family close behind her. She obviously thought the end had come. Imagine her expression when she saw her son sitting up in bed, weak and rather pale, but wondering what all the fuss was about!

It was a joyful scene, and it made Micki glow with happiness and pride for her part in it. It made her think of her own family all the more. But then she remembered that she'd never been introduced to Gregory, and she thought that after what he'd heard about his cousin Michelle, now was probably not the time.

Quietly, she managed to slip unobserved from the room. Though not before she heard Lizzie crooning delightedly, "Gregory's had a miracle! A miracle!"

14

The Tree Restored

Micki was certain she would be swept back to the twentieth century as soon as her task was finished. But she knew she would have to return from the lake. So without even waiting to say good-bye to Sarah, she slipped out of the house.

The first thing she noticed once she was outside was the tree. The ugly gash that had so disturbed her on her first day at the DeSilvers' had completely disappeared. In its place was spread out one of the broadest, strongest-looking limbs Micki had ever seen. It seemed impossible that it could ever collapse beneath the weight of a young boy.

Micki circled the tree curiously, running her fingers along its gnarled trunk. Suddenly she jumped back with a gasp of surprise. Her hand had touched something smooth but leathery.

"Well done, chicken!" The old woman's gray face had blended so perfectly with the silver trunk of the maple tree that Micki hadn't even noticed her. In fact, it almost seemed as if the woman had actually stepped out from inside the tree. The huge basket hung from her arm, and she carefully folded back the cloth that was draped over it.

"You wouldn't be going somewhere without returning a certain something, would you now?" She held out a gnarled hand. Micki hung her head. She knew the woman was referring to the stone egg, which she taken from Gregory's room and promptly secured in the pocket of her dress. But for some reason, she didn't wish to part with it. She had been hoping to keep it as a souvenir of her adventure. But the old woman shook her head firmly.

"Not advisable, chicken, believe me." Micki was about to argue when she remembered what her father had said about needing to have his stone egg with him wherever he went. It didn't sound very healthy. Better not take any chances, she thought. Besides, what choice did she have? She reached into her pocket and drew it out. It felt warm, as if some of its earlier glow still remained on the inside. Micki sighed and handed it over.

"Good girl," croaked the woman. "Now you needn't be running off so fast. I do believe someone is calling you. Take your time, Micki Silver. Remember, time is a funny thing."

"Michelle! Michelle!" Micki looked up to see Sarah leaning out of an upstairs window. "Where are you going? You must come back and meet Gregory! We've so much to tell him, haven't we?"

And so Micki did take her time.

The weeks went by, and she remained with the DeSilvers. She and Sarah became the best of friends. Also, slowly, she got to know Gregory. Slowly, because much as his recovery seemed a miracle, he did not get better overnight. It was many days before he was allowed out of bed, and Aunt Lydia, in her concern for his health, tended him constantly and allowed him only limited visiting privileges.

Aunt Lydia had decided not to engage another tutor until the end of the summer, and even her famous needlework sessions were few and far between. As a result, the girls were more or less left to do as they pleased. Everything was just as

Micki had pictured it—lazy days and cozy nights, merry games and shared secrets. Gradually they told Gregory bits and pieces of their story, and it was a favorite topic of his as he lay in bed regaining his strength.

Finally Gregory was allowed to get up, and after that his recovery was remarkably rapid. It wasn't long before he was joining Sarah and Micki in their games down by the lake. In fact, it was Gregory who challenged the girls to go for a swim on the first day of summer. The water was always quite cold at that time of year, explained Sarah, but it was a family ritual to usher in the warm weather.

It was not a particularly warm day. In fact it seemed to Micki that summer, which had seemed just around the corner back in April, had changed its mind and decided to put off making an appearance. But the family ritual was not to be denied, and together the three cousins set off for the lake with their bathing suits under their clothes. One could hardly call them suits, Micki thought with amusement—there was so much material it was almost like wearing another set of clothes.

When they reached the lake, both Sarah and Gregory lost no time in throwing off their clothes and running headlong into the water. Micki was far less enthusiastic, and she gingerly removed her pinafore and laid it, neatly folded, beneath the pine tree. Next came her shoes and stockings, which she placed next to her dress, taking particular care to line them up exactly. Slowly she made her way down to the lake's edge.

The first touch of the water was like an icy hand reaching out to grab her by the feet. She cried aloud at the shock and gazed in admiration at her cousins, whose bright blond heads were already bobbing about gaily above the surface of the lake.

"Come on, silly!" Sarah called. "You'll never have a swim at that rate. You have to plunge in all at once. Don't worry, it feels wonderful once you get all the way in."

Micki looked doubtful. The swimming pool they had at school was indoors and heated. And even when she'd swum in an unheated pool, it had been in the middle of the summertime with the hot July or August sun streaming down and warming up the water at the shallow end. She would always enter the pool there, easing her way down the stepladder. Then, once she was used to the temperature, she'd make her way to the cooler deep end of the pool.

But Sarah was calling to her insistently, telling her to stop acting like a baby. Micki felt she simply couldn't lose face in front of her cousins. Not after all they'd been through together.

She closed her eyes, took a deep breath, and hurled herself at the water. It closed over her like an ice coffin, pressing in on her head with a vise-like grip. Her heart pounded violently inside her chest. She tried to come up for air, but instead swallowed a mouthful of muddy water. Panic engulfed her, and she knew she was drowning.

She was awakened by a tremendous sneeze.

"Gesundheit!" Her father was beaming down at her. Micki realized that it was she who had sneezed. Her whole head seemed stuffed up.

"What happened?" she asked vaguely.

"I'd say you had a bit of a close call," replied her father. "As soon as we got back from the airport, you disappeared. I figured you were probably down at the lake. But when I came to look for you, I found you thrashing about in the water with all your clothes on. Micki, whatever possessed you to do such a thing?" he added severely.

"I . . . I can't remember. I guess I must have fallen in by accident."

At that moment the door burst open, and Jenny came barreling into the room, followed by her mother. Jenny jumped up on the bed and threw her arms around her sister.

"Micki, are you better?" she asked with concern. Micki smiled.

"Yes, I'm fine. Just a bit groggy."

"That's probably the medicine the doctor gave you to help you sleep," said her mother. "Micki, you gave us all quite a fright. You must promise *never* to do that again."

"I'm sorry, Mommy," she said, and began toying distractedly with the sheets. She was thinking of Sarah and Gregory, and how they must be feeling at this moment. She looked up to see Jenny gazing at her expectantly.

"What's wrong?" she asked. But Jenny apparently could contain herself no longer.

"Happy birthday, Micki!" she crowed triumphantly.

Happy birthday. Why, of course! It was Thursday. Micki had completely forgotten that she was to have her birthday while they were away at the lake. She was twelve years old today. She threw aside the bedclothes excitedly.

"It may be 'Happy Birthday,' but you're staying right where you are, young lady," said her mother firmly, tucking the sheets back in around her. "At least," she added, relenting, "until this evening. In the meantime, you get to have breakfast in bed. Your favorite—pancakes. Come on, Jenny, you can help me in the kitchen."

"I'm sorry you've got to stay in bed on your birthday, kitten," said her father sympathetically when her mother and Jenny had gone, "but it should give you time to read this." He handed Micki a large brown envelope. "I've been saving it for so long that I'd forgotten I had it. But I remembered when we went home yesterday, and brought it back. It was among my great-grandfather's papers when he died." Then, quietly, he left the room.

Micki examined the envelope. In faded ink were written the words, "For the eldest great-great-granddaughter of Gregory DeSilver. To be opened on her twelfth birthday." Micki tore open the envelope. Inside were several sheets of yellowed paper, covered on both sides with very cramped handwriting. The papers were wrapped neatly around a small box.

Micki unfolded the papers, and saw that they were pages of a letter addressed to her. The date on the letter was August 3, 1931.

"Dear Michelle," it read.

If you truly receive this letter on your twelfth birthday as I have intended, I will have been gone for many years. It will also mean that you have succeeded in your task of reinstating the DeSilver line. For I write to you as a man well past middle age. Thanks to you I survived the terrible thing that befell me when I was a lad of fifteen—a sickness that was nearly fatal.

It is many years now that I have been a married man and blessed with several children, including a son who has given me a grandson. Every day I thank God for sparing me my life. But I am cursed by the knowledge that this very life may cease to have been, snuffed out by a mysterious act that is to occur more than half a century from now.

It has occurred to me, as perhaps it will occur to you when you read this, that for my own self-interest, I should have arranged for you to receive this letter on your eleventh—rather than your twelfth—birthday, thereby attempting to avert that rash act that brought everything on. But several considerations have warned me against this.

First, it might happen that if my warning to you were to succeed, I might simply be taking events back to their starting point, bringing me no closer to my ultimate objective. For if you do refrain from the act and the accident never occurs, I will have no reason to ever write this letter, and thus unwarned, you would proceed as you have done.

Secondly, I say to myself, such an attempt at interference in the course of events may well be like a small twig trying to block the flow of a mighty river. For more likely than not you would have been confused by such a puzzling letter and simply have disregarded it.

My final reason lies in what I knew of you as my young cousin, and what perhaps is true of all of us: Telling you what to do or what not to do would be pointless. Thus, if this had been a letter of warning, rather than a letter of explanation, I feel quite sure you would have ignored it. Experience is truly the only teacher.

So this is, as I say, an explanation, a final rounding out of the tale. I am sure you will be interested in what became of those members of our family whose lives came together with yours for those brief months in the spring and summer of 1891.

My brother Matthew, who was a mere child when you knew him, and was, I believe, always my mother's favorite, grew to be a fine young man. But he was less fortunate than I, and in the summer of his nineteenth year he was stricken with typhoid and died shortly thereafter. So you see, I really was the only one able to carry on our family name.

Both Mary and Lizzie went on to happy

marriages with the sons of good families, and the three of us live close enough to see one another quite frequently and to watch our respective families grow together.

But I suspect it is really Sarah whose history holds most interest for you. The two of you were so strangely alike. No one could ever tell Sarah what to do or how to behave. When she was eighteen, she inherited a small amount of money from a doting aunt. With that modest financial independence she made her stand. She insisted on attending the music conservatory, much against our parents' wishes. Nevertheless, she did very well there, and became quite a celebrated concert pianist. As a result, Sarah has traveled all over the world, and only returns to see us on family occasions. I, for one, miss her a great deal, but am proud to have a sister whose name is known to so many.

And whatever happened to our cousin Michelle? That, of course, is the strangest story of all. I trust you remember that last time we were together at the lake on the first day of summer. Both Sarah and I saw you plunge into the water. We watched expectantly, but you didn't resurface. It was a moment of horror for us.

But then the oddest thing happened. I wouldn't have believed it but for Sarah's confirmation. For as we looked on, an apparition materialized. It was the dim outline of a man in a boat. He looked very much like my father. He rowed quite frantically to the spot where you had gone under, and reached his arm into the water. And out of the water he pulled a girl wearing trousers and an odd kind of jacket. The girl's outline was also very dim, but it did appear to be the image of you. She was spluttering and flailing her arms vigorously. Sarah called out "Michelle," but neither figure seemed to hear. Then they began to grow vaguer and vaguer, until they disappeared altogether.

Having to go back and tell our parents was awful, since we could never explain. They were deeply upset. They ordered the lake to be dragged, but of course no body was ever found. For a while, Sarah missed you terribly. She would lose herself for hours in her music. But eventually she realized it was best that you had returned to your own time and your own family.

Then there is the final mystery. That terrifying, magical old woman who could take on someone else's voice or put her own inside you; who seemed to fade in and out of the material world; who penetrated one's very dreams. Who was she? Was she some evil spirit come to wreak destruction on our family? Or was it she who was responsible for bringing about the happy resolution to our trials?

It is a question I have pondered for many years. And I think as I have grown older, my perspective has changed—one might say it has softened. For what seemed to me as a boy the embodiment of terror and all that was bad now seems no longer so. More than anything I believe that woman was a signpost rather than the road itself. She was there to show us the possibilities, the choices, and where our actions might lead us.

Well, so closes the chapter. But even in writing this I say to myself "How can you think such a thing? Have you learned nothing—the chapter is never closed." For who is to say that another hundred years after you are gone, some event may reverberate backward to change the course of your life, which will in its turn affect my own. Thus the entire cycle begins again, and its interconnections are endless. All we can do is live as we see best and accept responsibility for our own actions.

I feel terribly reluctant to end the final communication I will ever have with my cousin Michelle, so I forget that this is your twelfth birthday, and that you will most probably have far more exciting things to do on this day than to pore over the ramblings of a man getting on in years. I will therefore close by wishing you a happy and prosperous life and by thanking you once again for the gift of my own.

Sincerely,
Gregory DeSilver

P.S. When I last saw Sarah—this past Christmas at the old family mansion which I still call my home—I told her of my intention to write this letter to you. She came to me the very next day and begged me to enclose this with my letter. She said you would understand.

Micki turned the box over in her hands. It was long and flat and quite light. What had once been a smooth lacquer finish had now puckered with age, and much of it had fallen off in decay. The box was tied around several times with brown twine and fastened with a little brass latch. The string disintegrated into bits of sawdust as Micki unwound it.

She undid the latch and drew out a dank-smelling piece of cloth. It was stained and blotched with age, but there was no mistaking it. It was her sampler of long ago. Yet only yesterday she had been working on it. Crooked awkward stitches formed the words and letters:

Sticks and stones
Will brea

After this the letters changed to smaller, more neatly spaced stitches that completed the sampler.

Micki turned the sampler over and noticed that something was pinned to the back. It was a note on a folded piece of yellow paper.

Dear Michelle,
At least when you were around no one criticized my needlework.

S.

Micki lay back and sighed. Her great-great-great aunt Sarah was certainly long gone. It was hard to believe that she wouldn't see her impish grin again or hear her rallying everyone to some

212

new piece of mischief.

"Micki, Micki, can I come in?" called a tiny voice. The door opened slowly, and in walked Jenny proudly carrying a huge breakfast tray heaped with pancakes.

"Birthday breakfast," she announced gaily.

Micki grinned. It was going to be a wonderful birthday. And there was still more than a week left of her spring vacation.

About the Author

RUTH L. WILLIAMS grew up in Philadelphia, received a B.A. in English and Psychology from the University of Pennsylvania, and holds an M.B.A. from the Wharton School of Business. She has worked as an editor and proofreader for a medical publisher and for the encyclopedia division of a major publishing house. She currently lives in New York City and works for a public relations agency. This is her first book.